THE
STOLEN
TRAIN

THE STOLEN TRAIN

ROBERT ASHLEY

AN
APPLE
PAPERBACK

SCHOLASTIC INC.
New York Toronto London Auckland Sydney

ISBN 0-590-92150-9

12 11 10 9 8 7 6 5 4 3 2 1   6 7 8 9/9 0 1/0

Printed in the U.S.A.   40

First Scholastic printing, September 1996

To Arpy

Contents

THE STOLEN TRAIN

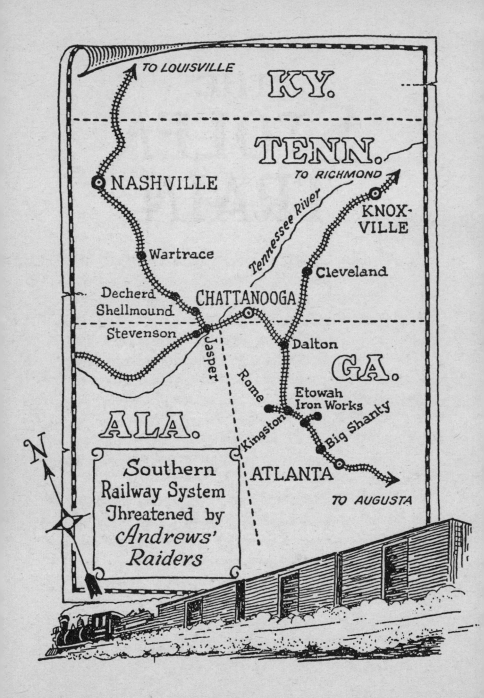

TO LOUISVILLE

KY.

TENN.

TO RICHMOND

NASHVILLE

Tennessee River

KNOX-VILLE

Wartrace

Cleveland

Decherd
Shellmound

CHATTANOOGA

Stevenson

Dalton

Jasper

GA.

Rome

Etowah
Iron Works

ALA.

Kingston

Big Shanty

N

Southern
Railway System
Threatened by
*Andrews'
Raiders*

ATLANTA

TO AUGUSTA

The Great Locomotive Chase

In the East, the first twelve months of the Civil War went badly for the Union Army. Soundly trounced at Bull Run in July, 1861, the Federals had been reorganized and whipped into shape by General McClellan, the Young Napoleon. But the Young Napoleon was a timid and hesitant field commander, ingenious at inventing excuses why he could not attack the enemy. As the war entered its second twelve months, McClellan had not yet taken decisive steps to besiege the Confederate capital at Richmond or to engage the Southern Army.

But in the West, President Lincoln had at least two leaders with a talent for rapid, determined action. One, of course, was "Unconditional Surrender" Grant; the other was a pint-sized general named Ormsby Mitchel. In the early months of 1862, General Grant captured forts Henry and Donelson, striking the first blows to gain control of the Mississippi River for the Union cause. About the same time, General Mitchel began a bold, swift movement toward the important Confederate railroad and supply center at Chattanooga, Tennessee. Capture of this city would isolate the Southern Army in the West and prevent the strengthening of the forces facing Grant.

On the evening of Sunday, April 6, a Federal espionage agent presented himself at General Mitchel's headquarters in Shelbyville, Tennessee. His name was James Andrews. He proposed a daring secret raid by disguised Union soldiers deep into Confederate territory. Their objective would be to immobilize the vital Western and Atlantic Railroad between Atlanta and Chattanooga. If successful, the raid would ensure the capture of Chattanooga by cutting the city off from supply and reinforcement. Andrews and Mitchel talked well into the morning, weighing the chances of success, poring over maps, and setting up a timetable. When the two men parted, they had agreed on a plan that involved the Andrews raiders in the stirring episode known as "the great locomotive chase." A chase is always exciting, but this one had the unique feature of being acted out not only by human participants but also by the two most famous locomotives of the Civil War, *The General* and *The Texas*.

The following is the story of *The General, The Texas*, and the Andrews raiders. The narrative is based on accounts by two of the raiders: *The Great Locomotive Chase,* by William Pittenger, and *The Adventures of Alf Wilson,* by James A. Wilson. With the exception of the boy hero, the raiders are historical characters. Likewise, the incidents described are historical, though somewhat telescoped in the interest of a more unified narrative.

R. A.

1.
A Secret Mission

The morning of April 7, 1862, began like every other morning Private Johnnie Adams had known since joining the Ohio Volunteers. Reveille had rudely shattered his blissful dreams of a warm, soft bed at home and a leisurely, tasteful breakfast in the kitchen with his mother. From reveille on, everything had followed the accustomed pattern: a tasteless breakfast hurriedly cooked over a fire in front of his tent and just as hurriedly eaten, assignment to the cleanup detail, two hours of drill under the hot midmorning sun, then another tasteless meal. After lunch, Johnnie had disappeared into his tent, unrolled his blanket, and lain down for an early afternoon nap. By now he had developed a pessimistic attitude about the length of these naps. Invariably his military superiors dreamed up some insignificant assignment and used it as an excuse to interrupt his siesta. The April 7 nap was no exception. But this time the interruption was for no trivial purpose.

Nor did the afternoon and evening of April 7 prolong the humdrum routine of the morning. Nor did the days that followed.

Johnnie had hardly closed his eyes after stretching out on his blanket, when the tent flap opened, a head popped in, and a voice said, "The Captain wants to see Private Adams."

Here we go again, thought Johnnie resignedly, rising slowly from his blanket. "What does he want this time?" he grumbled aloud.

"Haven't you heard?" said one of his tentmates. "General Mitchel's going to make you his aide."

"No, better'n that," said another mock-serious voice. "Abe Lincoln wants a new Secretary of War."

"Aw, shut up," said Johnnie disgustedly, clapping his kepi on his head and stumbling through the tent flap out into the bright noonday sun.

The orderly who had summoned Johnnie was walking rapidly past the long row of tents toward the Captain's quarters. Johnnie ran after him and, matching strides beside him, asked, "What's the Captain want me for?" The orderly shrugged his shoulders. Disappointed, Johnnie kept silent. The Company C parade grounds were practically deserted; nearly all the soldiers were napping in their tents. Lucky stiffs, Johnnie thought. Still, it wasn't everybody who got called by the Captain. Must be something more important than usual.

In a few minutes they reached the Company C

headquarters. The Captain was talking to a lieutenant. The orderly saluted. "Private Adams, sir." Johnnie saluted. "The Colonel wants to see you, Adams," the Captain said, turning and walking back in the direction from which Johnnie had just come. Johnnie obediently followed his company commander across the parade ground. What *is* this? he wondered. The Captain wants to see you. The Colonel wants to see you. Next it'll be the General wants to see you. Johnnie couldn't decide whether he was more bewildered, curious, irritated, or proud. After all, the Colonel didn't ask to see every soldier in the regiment. Still, you'd think they might tell a fellow what it was all about. You could ask an orderly, but not your company commander. Well, he'd just have to wait and see.

A group of men, both officers and soldiers, were gathered in front of the regimental headquarters. Johnnie recognized a few of them: Sergeant Marion Ross of Company A, Corporal William Pittenger of Company G, Private George Wilson of Company B, and Private Perry Shadrack of Company K. As Johnnie and the Captain came up, an aide detached himself from the group and went into the headquarters tent. In a few seconds he reappeared, followed by the regimental commander. The group snapped to attention and saluted. "Here's the man from Company C," the aide said to the Colonel. "They're all here now, sir."

6

"This one?" The Colonel looked at Johnnie a little doubtfully. "Are you sure he'll do?"

The Captain spoke up. "Yes, sir. He'll do. He's just what you asked for."

The Colonel nodded. "Very well, Captain." Then turning toward the group, "General Mitchel wants to see you men immediately."

Johnnie gulped. The General! He hadn't *really* expected to see the General. Pride now overmastered all other emotions. He had been a little hurt by the Colonel's question, but the Captain's reply had restored his self-esteem. He was just what the Colonel asked for. He still didn't know what the Colonel had asked for, but whatever it was, he was it. He supposed the General would clear up the mystery. Maybe one of the other men knew. As they started off toward the divisional headquarters, he fell in beside Corporal Pittenger.

"What's this all about, Pit?" he asked.

"Haven't the slightest idea," replied Pittenger. "Must be something big or we wouldn't be going to see the General."

They had now reached the divisional headquarters, a small wooden frame house. "Wait here, men," said the Colonel. He turned to an officer standing in front of the headquarters. "The men from the Second Regiment are here." The officer went into the house. A few moments later the door opened and out stepped a wiry, stern-looking little man wearing the single star of a brigadier general. It was Ormsby Mitchel, Commanding General of the Third Division, Army of the Ohio. The group came to attention and the Colonel saluted. "Here are the volunteers from the Second Regiment, General."

Johnnie's eyes popped. Volunteers! He hadn't volunteered for anything. Even a raw rookie like himself knew better than to do that. But the Colonel called them volunteers, so that was that.

"At ease," said General Mitchel, eyeing the "volunteers" sharply and, it seemed to Johnnie, not too approvingly. No wonder, thought Johnnie; they weren't a very impressive-looking group. General Mitchel's glance rested on Johnnie. "Who's this?" he snapped. Johnnie nearly jumped out of his skin. "I asked for men, not boys." Johnnie blushed, and then blushed again at having blushed the first time. He could hardly blame the General — he was only fifteen and didn't look much older. If the recruiting officer had been at all particular, he couldn't have enlisted, but at that time they were taking anybody who'd offer himself.

This time the regimental commander came to Johnnie's defense. "Begging your pardon, sir, you asked for a soldier who could run like a deer and climb like a monkey. Private Adams can do both." Once again Johnnie's heart swelled with pride. He was small, but he was tough, lithe, and wiry. He could beat anyone in the regiment at sprinting or climbing a greased pole.

General Mitchel grunted and turned to the next man, Pittenger. "What's he here for? He'd look better in a pulpit than in the army." Johnnie had to admit that General Mitchell was right. Pittenger, though strong and healthy, wore spectacles and looked like a scholar. Before the war he had taught school and studied law; after the war he planned to enter the ministry. Once again the Colonel came to the rescue.

"He has a mind like a steel trap, and he could talk his way into Jeff Davis' cabinet. He's a student of astronomy, too." This last was a shrewd touch, for Mitchel was probably the leading astronomer in America. He had been a professor of astronomy for most of his life after graduating from West Point, and he had built one of the first observatories in the country. Behind his back, his men called him "Old Stars."

"What difference does that make?" Mitchel snorted, but Johnnie could see that he was pleased as he passed on to Sergeant Ross. One look at Ross and the General's mood changed again. "Where does this fellow think he is? Parading down Fifth Avenue?" Again Johnnie could hardly blame Old Stars. Hair neatly brushed, beard carefully combed, every button polished to a bright shine, uniform immaculate — Ross could have stepped off the parade ground into a ballroom. "I suppose," said Mitchel dryly to the Colonel, "you can vouch for the Sergeant, too."

"Yes, sir. There's not a better noncom in the regiment." That satisfied Mitchel. He went on down the line, hurling taunts at each man and firing questions at the Colonel. Even Johnnie could see that he was testing each soldier, evaluating his fitness for some yet unrevealed mission. The little General fascinated Johnnie. Facially, he reminded Johnnie of the picture of Andrew Jackson hanging in the parlor back home. He had the same bushy gray hair, the same piercing eyes deep set beneath beetling brows, the same straight nose, the same determined lines about the mouth, and the same firm chin. You could hardly say that his soldiers loved him, but they certainly trusted him. He expected and got a high standard of performance from both soldiers and officers. In the short time since he had taken over the Third Division, he had shaped it into a first-class fighting unit.

His inspection over, General Mitchel nodded to the Colonel. "They'll do. No engineers?"

"No, sir," answered the Colonel.

"Too bad," said Mitchel. "Any in the other regiments?"

"Yes, sir. I think Colonel Neibling of the Twenty-first has a couple for you."

Mitchel now addressed himself to the soldiers standing at ease before him. "Men, you have volunteered for a secret mission of extreme importance to our cause." At the word "volunteered" there was a suggestion of a smile and a twinkle in the General's eye. So Old Stars has a sense of humor after all, Johnnie thought. The General continued. "This mission will place you in the greatest personal danger. You will wear civilian clothes and go deep into enemy territory. It is only fair to warn you that if caught you may be hanged as spies. No one is under orders to accept a role in this undertaking. If you do not wish to go, you may back out honorably by so informing your company commander. If you do wish to go, you are to purchase civilian clothes in Shelbyville this afternoon. You are also to provide yourselves with pistols, but no other weapons. Get yourselves a couple days' rations. Do not carry on your person any mail or other identifying papers.

"Whether you decide to go or not, the utmost secrecy must be preserved. You are to say nothing about the mission to anyone outside this group. Men are also being selected from the other two Ohio regiments in Colonel Sill's brigade, and you may see them in Shelbyville. But you are not to discuss the mission with them.

"Your leader is Mr. James Andrews. I trust him implicitly. You will meet him shortly after dark tonight on the Wartrace road a mile or so out of town.

"I can tell you no more. All further information

11

will come from your leader." General Mitchel turned on his heel and disappeared into his headquarters.

That night at dusk Johnnie, Ross, and Pittenger left Shelbyville, a small Tennessee town a short distance from camp, and started down the road to Wartrace. For a few minutes the three soldiers walked on quietly, each busy with his own thoughts. Finally, Ross broke the silence. "Who's this Andrews?"

Johnnie didn't know, but Pittenger did. "A secret agent working for the Army of the Ohio, one of the best in the business. He's made several trips deep into Southern territory."

"Several trips?" Ross was amazed. "Those fellows usually don't last that long. Two or three trips and they're caught. Or they decide to quit before their luck runs out. How's he lasted so long?"

"He's a Southerner, native son of Virginia, adopted son of Kentucky. He's every inch the Southern gentleman — that tends to lull suspicion."

Ross persisted. "I still don't see how he's survived several secret missions."

"He's worked out a foolproof system. Poses as a Southern sympathizer and land blockade-runner. Smuggles medical supplies into the South. That guarantees him passage through the Confederate lines. His trips back north to get more supplies

12

give him the opportunity to relay information to the Union generals without exciting the suspicions of his Confederate friends. As long as he carries medical goods to the South, the Confederates won't touch him. If he gets picked up by Northern soldiers, he can refer his captors to his Union superiors. Pretty ingenious, a Union secret agent posing as a Confederate secret agent."

Ross wasn't convinced. "He'll play his string out and get caught one of these days. Just our luck to have him fail this time and drag us down with him. I don't like the way this thing has been planned. 'Meet Mr. Andrews on the Wartrace road a mile or two out of town shortly after dark.' Pretty vague. We don't even know what Andrews looks like."

"Anyone who isn't smart enough to find Andrews isn't smart enough to go on the mission. We're being tested before it's too late," replied Pittenger.

Johnnie spoke for the first time. "I wonder what the mission is."

"Something that involves the skill of engineers and your knack for running and climbing," said Pittenger.

"Yeah, but what kind of engineers?" asked Ross.

"Locomotive engineers is my guess. Andrews has just returned from an attempt to seize a train on the Western and Atlantic Railroad. He had eight men from Company C disguised as Southern citizens. They were going to capture a locomotive near Atlanta and take it north to Chattanooga, burning bridges, tearing up track, and cutting telegraph wires. An engineer on the railroad whom Andrews knew as a Union sympathizer was going to run the locomotive for him. He never showed up, so they had to abandon the scheme."

"It wouldn't have worked anyhow," was Ross's comment.

"Maybe not. But Andrews thought it would and probably still thinks so. If I were a betting man, I'd wager a week's pay that Andrews is going to try again, but this time he's going to take his own engineers with him. That's why Old Stars asked the Colonel if we had any engineers in the regiment."

"It still won't work," Ross muttered.

None of Ross's objections carried any weight with Johnnie. He was beside himself with excitement. To go in disguise deep into Confederate territory! Steal a train right out from under the noses of the Johnny Rebs! Make a mad dash north, burning bridges, tearing up track, and cutting telegraph wires! Telegraph wires — maybe that's where he came in! Maybe he had been chosen to shinny up poles and cut the wires! What an experience for a fifteen-year-old boy!

It was now dark. Rain was beginning to fall. A high wind had risen and was driving storm clouds across the sky. At frequent intervals and for long periods of time, the moon was blacked out and the three soldiers walked along in complete darkness broken only by intermittent flashes of lightning. The rain fell with increasing violence, turning the dirt road into a treacherous quagmire. Especially in the intervals of darkness, it was difficult for them to keep their footing, and more than once Johnnie nearly tumbled into the ditch beside the road. He was happy to have company, for the loneliness of the road, the blackness of the night, the rumble of the thunder, the flashing of the lightning, and the howling of the wind through the trees sent shivers down his spine that were not caused by the chill wet of the evening.

"How are we going to find Andrews on a night like this?" asked Ross.

"Maybe we've gone too far. Let's turn back," suggested Pittenger. Suddenly a brilliant flash of lightning lit up the road and revealed a muffled figure standing before a grove of trees. It was Perry Shadrack.

"Hey!" he said. "In here."

2.
James J. Andrews

From beneath his coat, Shadrack pulled a lantern. Guided by its dim light, Johnnie and his friends made their way along a faintly marked path. "Would have missed you except for that flash of lightning," said Shadrack.

"You can't see your hand in front of your face on a night like this," remarked Ross. "Everybody else here?"

"Dunno. Most everybody, I guess."

The trail began to slope upward. Johnnie thought he could hear a hum of voices. The hum grew louder. Suddenly Shadrack stopped.

"Three more, Mr. Andrews. Sergeant Ross, Corporal Pittenger, and Private Adams, all from the Second Ohio."

"That makes twenty-four," said a voice which Johnnie judged to be Andrews'. "Everybody's here now." In a louder voice, "Gather around, gentlemen."

Johnnie heard the rustling of wet clothes and

the shuffling of feet. Shadrack had moved to Andrews' side and was holding the lantern aloft. The moon had broken through the clouds. Johnnie saw that they were in a small clearing on the top of a gentle rise of ground. There was Andrews, erect, dignified, and self-possessed. He was a man in his mid-thirties, about six feet tall, strongly built. Regular features and a luxuriant beard covering the lower half of his face made him decidedly handsome. His voice and manner were quiet and refined, yet firm. Johnnie wondered what in Andrews' past had put the look of sadness in his eyes. Around him were arranged the "volunteers" in an odd assortment of civilian clothing, hat brims pulled down, coat collars turned up, and shoulders hunched. Johnnie wondered how many regretted "volunteering" and wished they were back in the comparative comfort of their tents at Shelbyville. He, for one, had no such wish, even though he would hardly have been wetter if he had jumped into the Ohio River with his clothes on. He listened eagerly to Andrews.

"You men know that you have been selected for a hazardous secret mission that will take you deep into Confederate territory, but unless there has been some shrewd guessing, that is all you know." An ear-splitting crash of thunder silenced Andrews momentarily. It was now dark again. Storm clouds had once more obscured the moon, and Shadrack had either doused his lantern or hidden it beneath his coat. As Andrews went on, an owl hooted mournfully and a dog howled eerily in the distance. Shivers raced down Johnnie's spine.

"The success of this mission may mean the loss of Tennessee, even of the whole West, to the Confederacy. You all know that Chattanooga is the key to the situation. At present it is weakly defended and will probably fall to General Mitchel, *unless*" — Andrews paused dramatically — "unless General Leadbetter can get reinforcements. Right now, reinforcements can reach Chattanooga by rail from the west, the south, and the northeast. Tomorrow morning General Mitchel moves south into Alabama with the object of seizing Huntsville on the Memphis-Charleston Railroad, the main line to the west. That will eliminate the possibility of reinforcements from General Beauregard at Corinth. To the northeast, our General Morgan is strong enough to contain General Kirby Smith in Knoxville. That means no reinforcements from that direction. If Leadbetter is to get reinforcements, he must get them from the south. It is our job to see that he does not."

A murmur of surprise and excitement swept through the group of men gathered around Andrews. Johnnie gasped. None of his wildest dreams of romantic adventure had envisioned a mission of such strategic importance.

Andrews continued in his steady, quiet, cultured tone. "Reinforcements from the south must

18

pass over the Western and Atlantic Railroad running from Atlanta to Chattanooga. If the Western and Atlantic is destroyed, Leadbetter will not be reinforced." Another clap of thunder made Andrews pause. The rain was still falling in sheets.

"Some of you may have heard that I have just returned from an attempt to seize a train between Atlanta and Chattanooga. I failed because my engineer, a Union sympathizer employed by the railroad, was transferred to the West and could not make the rendezvous. I had no one with me who could run a locomotive. But I mean to try again, and I do not intend to fail. This time I am taking my own engineers — three of them, William Knight, Wilson Brown, and Martin Hawkins.

"My plan is to seize a train near the southern end of the line and run it north, burning bridges, tearing up track, and cutting telegraph lines as we go. If we succeed, we'll roar right through Chattanooga and on to Bridgeport in Alabama. There we will meet General Mitchel, who will bring most of his army up from Huntsville on the Memphis-Charleston tracks. When we meet there, we will have cut the Confederacy in two. General Beauregard will be isolated in Mississippi and General Smith will be marooned in Knoxville. Chattanooga and all Tennessee will fall to Mitchel." Andrews raised his usually calm and steady voice. A note of elation elevated his tone. "You men can shorten the war by months." The moon emerged from the clouds and lit the clearing with sudden brilliance. Johnnie could see that Andrews' features were flushed with excitement. "Are there any questions?" Andrews asked.

Johnnie was not surprised to hear Ross speak up.

"Yes, Mr. Andrews, I'd like to know how you plan to seize the train." There was a hint of distrust in the Sergeant's voice.

"I'd rather not tell you now. I'll outline specific plans at our next meeting. Any more questions?" No one spoke. In the silence that followed, Johnnie heard the dog still howling in the distance. The moon again went behind the clouds, and darkness gradually obscured the little group. Andrews resumed. "Now a word about the danger and the difficulty of the mission. Our raid will take us well within the Southern lines. Some of you may be captured. Since you will be soldiers traveling as civilians, you may be treated as spies. You know the penalty." Johnnie's neck felt a little uncomfortable. "I tell you this since it is not too late for you to withdraw from the mission if you so desire. You may depart in the darkness without prejudice to your military record. I have General Mitchel's word for that." Andrews paused, but no one made a move to leave.

"We are all willing to risk our lives, Mr. Andrews, if we feel that our raid has a good chance of succeeding. What *are* our chances?" It was Ross again.

"Well, sir, if I didn't think our chances were pretty good, I wouldn't risk my own life and the lives of twenty men." Good for Andrews, thought Johnnie; maybe that will silence Ross for a while. Again there was a pause. Andrews was giving the "volunteers" every chance to back out. There was a shuffling of feet, but no one left.

"Good," said Andrews. "I see that General Mitchel has chosen his men well. You were all picked because of some special talent or quality you possess. You will all have particular assignments to carry out. What they are you will learn at our rendezvous behind the Confederate lines."

"Where is that?" It was Ross again. His voice showed his irritation and impatience at Andrews' vagueness.

"Marietta, Georgia." A gasp of astonishment rose from the group of soldiers.

"Marietta!" exclaimed Ross.

"That's right," replied Andrews calmly.

"But that's in the heart of the Confederacy, over two hundred miles from here!" protested Ross.

"I know that," said Andrews in the same even tone.

"How do we get there?" Ross persisted.

"You will divide into small groups of not more than four men. You will make your way southeast through the Cumberland Mountains and across the Tennessee River to Chattanooga. You must be there no later than the afternoon of Thursday the tenth. You will be traveling in rough and mountainous country. Unless this weather breaks soon, the streams will be swollen and you may have difficulty getting across. I know it won't be easy; but you will have nearly four days to make the trip, and I think you can do it. You'll have to, because the last train leaves Chattanooga for Marietta at three P.M., and you must be in Marietta that night."

The moon was still behind the clouds, but the lightning flashed with increasing frequency, bathing the clearing in a lurid light nearly as bright as day. During these brief intervals, Johnnie could see the calm features of Andrews and the tense faces of the little group of men gathered around him. With each crash of thunder, Andrews paused so that his men would miss none of his instructions.

"Mr. Andrews, how do you suggest we travel?" This time it was Pittenger, speaking with a deference in striking contrast to Ross's aggressiveness.

"You may travel any way you wish — on foot, by railroad, or in wagons. I will give you plenty of Confederate money, so that you will be able to buy train tickets or hire wagons, as well as pay for food and lodging. Of course you will leave here on foot. Just over the clearing you will find the single track that runs eight miles from Shelbyville to Wartrace.

You can follow it to the Nashville and Chattanooga Railroad and then strike out across country. Head east for Manchester, then start working southeast through Hillsboro, Tracy City, and Jasper toward the Tennessee River. If you wish, you may double back toward the Nashville-Chattanooga tracks and ride the rails from Shellmound to Chattanooga. Stay in your original groups. If your paths cross, don't show any signs of recognition unless you are sure you are not watched. Above all, don't speak to me, if you happen to meet me."

"What shall we say if we are asked where we are going and why?" asked a man behind Johnnie.

"Say that you are Kentuckians escaping from the Yankees and traveling south to enlist in the Confederate Army. If you cross the Nashville-Chattanooga tracks and head east and then southeast, you will appear to be coming from Kentucky rather than from the Union armies to the west. You can say that you are searching for a particular Kentucky regiment in which you wish to serve. Speak as little as possible, for your Northern accents may betray you."

"But suppose our stories don't work?" asked the voice behind Johnnie.

"In that case the best thing to do is enlist on the spot. It will be better to serve in the Southern Army for a while than to risk discovery of our plans by being too stubborn about enlisting somewhere else. You can probably escape some dark night while you are on picket duty. If you are discovered in the Confederate Army, General Mitchel will see that you are not charged with desertion."

"But will they take us if they are suspicious?" asked Pittenger.

There was a hint of amusement in Andrews' reply. "The difficulty is to stay out of the Southern Army, not to get into it. They'll take anyone these days. Even the jails are being emptied to secure conscripts. As long as they don't suspect you of being Union soldiers, they'll sign you up. If by any chance they become convinced you are disguised soldiers and you cannot shake their conviction, then you must say you are acting under orders. Never admit that you had a chance to back out or that you knew the nature of our mission. Then you may be treated as prisoners of war. Any more questions?"

No one spoke. As Andrews went on, his voice again had an exalted tone. "We are about to embark on a thrilling and dangerous mission. The risks are great, but the stakes are high. We may not succeed; but if we do, how glorious will be our accomplishment! Just imagine! To steal a train right out from under Confederate noses and run it through one hundred miles of Confederate territory, tearing up their track, cutting their telegraph, burning their bridges! We will deal the enemy the deadliest blow of the war! Tennessee and all the West will be ours!" Johnnie thrilled to his leader's words, and he was sure that the older men about him also caught the speaker's enthusiasm.

"All right, boys" — Andrews was his usual self again — "split up into groups. I want the older men mixed with the younger. Knight, Brown, and Hawkins, join different groups — I can't risk having my engineers all caught at once. When you are organized, report to me for your Confederate money. The groups will leave at intervals of fifteen minutes. That's all."

As the men began to separate into small units, the moon bathed the clearing in a flood of brilliance. "Well," said Pittenger, "we already have a group of three. Let's report to Andrews."

"No, Pit," said Ross, "if you don't mind, I'm going to ask to accompany Andrews."

Pittenger looked at Ross sharply. "Still don't trust him, eh, Marion?"

"I'd follow him to the ends of the earth," Johnnie broke in enthusiastically.

"I wouldn't follow anyone there, unless I was sure he knew his way, and I'm not sure Andrews does," Ross retorted.

As Ross walked toward Andrews, the soldier behind Johnnie spoke up. "Alf Wilson and I will join you, if you'll have us. I'm Bill Knight." So the voice behind him belonged to Knight, the engineer.

"Glad to have you," said Pittenger. "Let's go."

There must be two Wilsons among the raiders, thought Johnnie: George Wilson from the Second and their new companion, Alf.

The four soldiers made their way to their leader. "We have a group ready, Mr. Andrews," said Knight. Andrews scrutinized the men closely, nodded his approval, and began counting out money.

"Here's thirty dollars in Confederate bills for each of you. Keep cool and use your heads, boys, and everything will turn out right. Remember, be in Marietta on the night of the tenth." Andrews was now counting out Johnnie's money. "Good luck, Johnnie," he said kindly.

"Thank you, sir," Johnnie replied, wondering how Andrews knew who he was. Ross, standing beside Andrews, waved to Johnnie and Pittenger.

As Johnnie turned to follow his three companions, the moon disappeared beneath a cloud, blotting out Andrews and the rest of the party. Knight led the way out of the clearing. They had gone a few yards down the incline when a sudden flash of lightning lit up the scene. Johnnie looked over his shoulder. There was Andrews, tall, erect, calm, and dignified, addressing another group. Suddenly, all was dark again. Johnnie stumbled after Knight.

3.
Rendezvous at Marietta

Johnnie and his companions reached Marietta several hours ahead of schedule on Thursday, the tenth of April. They owed their early arrival to Knight's insistence on traveling by rail. Knight had the railroader's contempt for foot travel and could see no point in trudging over muddy country roads, wading through swollen streams, and climbing up rugged mountainsides when only a few miles away was a perfectly reliable railroad that would take them quickly and comfortably to their destination. After two days of following the overland route suggested by Andrews, Knight had proposed that they head south until they hit the tracks of the Nashville and Chattanooga Railroad, and there take a train for Chattanooga. When Pittenger pointed out that this was a violation of Andrews' instructions, Knight retorted that only by taking a train could they reach Marietta on Thursday — half their allotted traveling time had elapsed, but they had covered less than a quarter of the distance to their rendezvous. This silenced all objection. The four soldiers headed south for the junction town of Decherd and boarded an express which got them to Chattanooga shortly after 9:00 P.M. on Wednesday. There was no sign of Andrews or the rest of the party.

After a night's sleep at the Crutchfield House across the street from the depot, they decided to take the morning train for Marietta rather than the afternoon train mentioned by Andrews. Knight wanted to travel by daylight so that he could become somewhat familiar with the route over which he was to pilot a stolen locomotive. Arriving in Marietta at 3:30, they registered under assumed names at the railroad hotel near the depot. Finding none of the party there, Knight sent Johnnie into town to check the other hotel. But there was no sign of the raiders in town, either.

At 11:30 the four soldiers gathered on the platform to meet the train Andrews had cautioned everyone not to miss. "If you see any of the party, don't speak to them till we get back to the hotel," warned Knight. A few minutes later, a whistle eerily broke the stillness of the night. In the distance rails glistened. Then the engine, pouring black smoke from its stack, came slowly around the bend. The stationmaster emerged from the depot carrying a lantern. "On time," he remarked.

The train clanked to a halt, brakes grinding and steam escaping from the cylinders. The sleepy coaches came to life momentarily, then relapsed into sleep again. One passenger descended. It was not one of the raiders. A second passenger, then a third, but still no sign of Andrews and his men. The train laboriously pulled away. The stationmaster disappeared. The depot was deserted except for Johnnie and his comrades. They met in the center of the platform.

"Something's gone wrong," said Pittenger uneasily.

"Sure has," agreed Knight, nodding slowly. "This infernal weather must have delayed our friends so they couldn't get to Chattanooga today."

Johnnie's chief worry was that the raid might be canceled. "Can we still steal the train tomorrow?" he asked anxiously.

"We can, provided Old Stars is held up by the weather, too. If he isn't, then we're in for trouble. If he takes Huntsville tomorrow morning, then the single track from Chattanooga to Atlanta will be crowded with southbound refugee trains fleeing Mitchel's advance and with northbound troop trains carrying reinforcements to Chattanooga. We'll have one devil of a time trying to run a stolen train northward over a crowded single track, especially when the whole countryside will be alerted.

The success of our plan depends on timing. We should be starting north about the same time Old Stars takes Huntsville."

"I hope you're wrong," said Pittenger.

"I'm not," Knight insisted. "I'm only telling you what Old Stars told me when I was chosen as one of the engineers."

"Then," said Wilson, "our only hope is that Mitchel has been delayed, too."

"Count that out," said Pittenger. "If General Mitchel said he'd take Huntsville early Friday morning, he will. He'll march his troops all night if necessary. He'll be in Huntsville tomorrow morning."

"Maybe Andrews realizes this and has called the raid off," said Wilson.

"Perhaps," said Knight. "We'll just have to wait around tomorrow and see if Andrews shows up. If he doesn't, then we'll quit and head for home."

Andrews and his raiders were not on the early morning train, nor on the afternoon express. But the stationmaster had some important information for them. "Bad news from the West," he said as the afternoon train pulled away from the station. "The Yanks have occupied Huntsville. Captured about fifteen engines and seventy-five cars. They say Mitchel is moving toward Stevenson and hopes to take Chattanooga. That means a busy day for me tomorrow. Probably be several specials

30

going both ways on the single track. You fellows expecting someone?"

"Yes," answered Pittenger quickly. "We're supposed to meet a friend from home. Should have been here yesterday. Hope nothing's happened to him."

"Where you from?"

"Kentucky. Our friend's arranged for us to join a Kentucky regiment."

"Oh, Kentuckians. Thought for a minute you might be Yankees. Accent didn't sound right."

"No, we're not Yanks. Some people up home are, but we're not."

"Well, good luck. Maybe your friend will be on the late train."

"Hope so. If he isn't, I guess we'll head back to Chattanooga and enlist. Maybe we can help keep old Mitchel out of the city."

Once again the four Union men walked up the road to the railroad hotel. "Phew!" said Knight, wiping his forehead. "That guy's getting too nosy. You handled him nicely, Pit. What a spy you'd make!" Knight laughed. By now Johnnie had learned that a wry sense of humor was one of Knight's outstanding traits. Like Wilson, Knight was in his late twenties, nearly twice as old as Johnnie. He had a strong, sturdy build and a broad, pleasant face. A devoted railroader, he had had three years' experience as an engineer in Ohio and western Pennsylvania before joining the Union

31

Army. His fireman, Alf Wilson, was short, slender, and wiry; soft-spoken and deliberate; slow to speak and slow to act, but determined and tenacious as a bulldog once his mind was made up. Wilson, Knight, Pittenger — Johnnie was proud to be the fourth member of the quartet.

"We better be careful tonight," said Pittenger. "If the rest of the party comes, we can't speak to anyone 'cept Andrews. My story won't hold water if we seem to belong to a large group."

"All right, Pit," agreed Knight. "We'll let you do the talking. But if you ask me, Andrews won't be on the train. Even if he is, our goose is cooked. That news about Huntsville does it."

"Don't give up yet," advised Pittenger. "Let's see what the midnight train brings. Maybe Andrews has something figured out."

"Okay, Pit. But it's a shame we didn't steal the train today. Perfect weather for bridge burning — the only sunny day we've had this week. But there's no use crying over spilled milk. Let's get some sleep."

When they assembled on the platform again that night, Johnnie had his fingers crossed. He hoped with all his might for Andrews to be on the midnight train. Once more the whistle in the distance, the light on the tracks, the huge engine puffing and wheezing around the bend and grinding to a stop, the stir of activity in the coaches, the descent of a few sleepy passengers. Johnnie could feel his heart pounding in his chest. Then it leaped to his throat. Down there, getting off the last coach — that tall, commanding figure in the silk hat — there was no mistaking him! It was Andrews! Johnnie could have shouted with joy. He was sure everything would be all right now — Andrews would have the answer. Johnnie started to run toward his leader. But suddenly he saw that Pittenger was talking to another of the passengers — it was Ross. Remembering Pit's warning about speaking to only one of their comrades, he checked himself and walked toward the two men from the Second Ohio. He wondered why Pittenger had approached Ross rather than Andrews, but decided that he had simply seen the Sergeant first. Wilson and Knight were already there when Johnnie reached his two friends.

"Good to see you fellows. We thought we'd lost you. Andrews was plenty worried, especially about you, Knight. He didn't fancy losing one of his engineers. Hi, Johnnie."

"You worried about us!" snorted Pittenger. "What do you think we've been having here, a tea party? Where've you all been? We got here yesterday afternoon."

"Held up by the weather. Soon's Andrews realized we couldn't make Chattanooga on Thursday, he passed the word to postpone the raid for a day.

We all came down together tonight. Didn't you get the word?"

"No, we haven't laid eyes on any of the party till now."

Johnnie could contain himself no longer. "Then the raid's still on?"

"Sure is, Johnnie."

Knight broke in. "I s'pose you've heard that Mitchel took Huntsville this morning?"

"Yeah, we heard," said Ross quietly.

"But that ruins our timing. We should've been moving toward Chattanooga when Mitchel took Huntsville."

"Andrews knows that, but he's going to chance it anyhow."

"You seem to have changed your opinion of Andrews," remarked Pittenger.

"You're right, Pit. I'd follow that man to the ends of the earth."

"Johnnie said that several days ago, Marion," Pittenger commented dryly.

"I know he did, Pit. Don't rub it in."

Knight was still anxious about the morrow. "What are Andrews' plans?" he asked.

"We meet in his room at dawn. He'll give us final instructions then. Leave word with the clerk to wake you in the morning. I'll let you know later the number of Andrews' room. Say, how'd you fellas make such good time?"

"We flew," remarked Alf Wilson.

Pittenger laughed. "Knight doesn't like to walk. We boarded a train at Decherd. Rode all the way except for the first thirty miles. Nothing like brains, you know."

"Nothing like disobeying orders you mean."

Soon they reached the hotel. In the lobby Johnnie saw George Wilson and Perry Shadrack. The rest he did not know. After leaving the call time with the clerk, Johnnie and Pit climbed the stairs to their room. As they were undressing, Ross stuck his head in the door. "Room seven at dawn."

At four the next morning, Johnnie and Pittenger knocked at Room seven. Andrews opened the door himself. "Hello, Johnnie. Corporal Pittenger," he said, shaking hands with both of them. "It's good to see you. Come in."

Andrews closed the door. Johnnie saw that the room was filled with men — about twenty was his guess — some on chairs, some standing, some on Andrews' bed. Andrews turned toward his men, his back against the door. "Everyone's here, I believe, except Porter and Hawkins."

"They're staying at the hotel in town, sir. Couldn't get rooms here," said Ross.

"We'd better begin. They'll probably be along soon." Andrews paused. "Boys," he continued, speaking in a low tone so as not to be heard outside the room, "you've come through in fine style. Not counting Porter and Hawkins, we're missing only two men of the group that left Shelbyville Monday night. That gives us twenty men plus Porter and Hawkins — plenty for the job."

Andrews paused again. The room was tense with expectation. No one spoke or moved. Andrews continued. "But the dangers and hardships and difficulties you've faced up to now are nothing to what you will face from now on. This morning we put our plan in operation. Within two hours we seize our engine and start moving north."

Johnnie's throat choked. Several men leaned forward in their excitement. Others smiled and nodded.

"The early morning mail for Chattanooga reaches here at five twenty-five. When it leaves, we shall all be aboard. You are to go to the depot in small groups at intervals of a few minutes. Do not communicate with other groups. Buy tickets for any station along the way.

"The mail will be pulled by a fine new engine, *The General* — we couldn't ask for a handsomer gift from Jeff Davis." Andrews smiled at his little joke. "Behind the tender will be three empty boxcars, a baggage car, and two coaches. The conductor is William Fuller. He's a capable man and he's been alerted to look for deserters, so don't arouse his suspicions." Once again, Johnnie was amazed at Andrews' store of information. How did he know the name of the engine, the capabilities of the conductor, and the number and kind of cars that would make up the train? "You will all board the forward coach. A half-hour later the train will stop at Big Shanty. You will remain in your seats till I give the signal. When I do, we will seize the train."

"But why Big Shanty, Mr. Andrews?" asked Knight.

"Two reasons, Mr. Knight. First, Big Shanty is the breakfast stop. The train will be there for twenty minutes. The passengers and the train crew will get off for breakfast. That will leave the engine unguarded — it will be ours for the taking.

"Second, Big Shanty has no telegraph office. There is no way that pursuit can be quickly and effectively organized. The nearest engines are at Atlanta, thirty miles to the south, and at Kingston, thirty miles to the north. To get help from Atlanta, the Confederates will have to send a man on horseback through the hills to Marietta. By the time he can telegraph a message to Atlanta, we'll have a two-hour start on any pursuing locomotive from the south. If they send a man north to the nearest telegraph station, he will find that we have cut the wires and he will have to ride all the way to Kingston. Again we'll have a two-hour start on any pursuit by rail."

Johnnie was elated. They couldn't miss. His admiration for Andrews reached new heights. What a plan!

"But," Knight persisted, "Camp McDonald's

right beside the track at Big Shanty. There'll be ten thousand Confederate soldiers watching the train."

Johnnie gasped. He hadn't thought of that. The scheme didn't sound so airtight now. How could they get by the troops?

"They won't pay any attention to us," answered Andrews. "Their very numbers will be to our advantage. They'll never dream of a train theft. And remember we'll reach Big Shanty about six o'clock. The camp will be barely awake, and the soldiers will be busy with breakfast." Johnnie nodded. Andrews was making it sound easy again.

Andrews continued: "When I give the signal, you'll get off on the left side, the camp side, of the tracks. Brown, Knight, Adams, Wilson, and I will take possession of the cab. The rest of you will pile into the boxcars and slide the doors to." Johnnie was beside himself. Like all boys, he had always dreamed of riding a locomotive cab. What a time to have his dream come true!

"Suppose someone tries to stop us." It was Ross this time.

"You all have pistols," said Andrews soberly. "If necessary, use them. But only as a last resort. We don't want our plans revealed too soon. A pistol shot will bring the entire camp down on our heads. But if you have to, shoot!

"As we move northward, we'll tear up track at convenient intervals. Just out of sight of each sta-

38

tion, we'll stop to cut telegraph wire, in case anyone gets suspicious and decides to send a message ahead. But our main object will be to burn the three big bridges near Chattanooga — one over the Oostanaula River and two over Chickamauga Creek."

"That'll be hard to do if we get any more rain," remarked Pittenger.

"With all the rain we've had in the past few days, we're due for some good weather."

Andrews paused before going on. "You have all been picked for particular abilities and to perform particular tasks. Knight and Brown will serve as engineers. When they need relief, we'll call on Hawkins; that is, if he gets here in time. Alf Wilson is our fireman. Johnnie Adams will be my lookout and my messenger boy — he's small and agile enough to clamber all over the train, even at top speed. And when we stop, we'll send Johnnie up the poles to cut the wires for us." So that was why he had been chosen!

"What about tools?" asked Ross.

"That poses a problem. I have a small saw and a couple hammers. George Wilson has some axes in his carpetbag. Rail-lifting equipment we'll have to pick up along the way."

"Suppose people begin asking questions when we have to stop for wood and water?" asked Pittenger.

"We pose as a powder train running supplies to

General Beauregard. I have a signed pass from the Confederate General to that effect. Let me do the talking. You men in the boxcars must stay behind closed doors except when otherwise ordered. No one must know that I'm carrying human cargo rather than kegs of powder. Anyone else with questions?"

"Not a question, Mr. Andrews," said Ross in a sober tone. "But I'd like to suggest that we call the whole thing off." Johnnie was astonished. So Ross still had doubts about the raid, even though he had full faith in Andrews. But Johnnie noticed that the Sergeant's tone was respectful, without a trace of the aggressiveness that had marked his questioning of Andrews back in Shelbyville.

"Why, Sergeant?" asked Andrews.

"Well, sir, it seems to me that the success of our plans depended on our working together with General Mitchel. Through no fault of ours, we're a day behind schedule. We should have moved north as General Mitchel took Huntsville. But he took it yesterday. Now the whole countryside is aroused. The single track will be crowded with special trains. We'll have to spend too much time on sidings waiting for the track to clear. Every minute we lose that way will be time gained for the organization of a pursuit."

"I think Ross is right," said Knight.

"So do I," said Alf Wilson.

"He has raised a valid objection," admitted Andrews. "But I think the day's delay may even work to our advantage. In the confusion aroused by Mitchel's advance, it will be much easier for us to pose as a powder train. We'll be merely one of several trains not normally scheduled for the Atlanta-Chattanooga run.

"Boys, I've tried this once and failed. This time I'll succeed or leave my bones in Dixie!"

4.
A New Crew for
The General

It was 5:20 when Johnnie joined the line forming at the ticket window in the Marietta station. As he reached the head of the line and ordered a ticket for Allatoona — he liked the sound of the name — a whistle hooted in the distance. Johnnie grabbed his ticket and ran out to the platform. Down the track the train had just rounded the bend and was slowing down on the straight stretch leading to the depot. As the gleaming black engine moved ponderously past him, Johnnie gazed admiringly at its pointed cowcatcher, its rectangular headlight, its funnel-shaped stack, and its two huge driving wheels. On the boiler was a bright gold nameplate inscribed with the single word "General." Behind the tender, which bore the number "3" and the letters "W & A R R," were the boxcars Andrews had mentioned, the baggage car, and the two coaches. Remembering Andrews' instructions, Johnnie boarded the forward coach and walked down the aisle toward the front of the car. Andrews had taken a seat on the right-hand side; next to him was Perry Shadrack. Pittenger and Ross were across the aisle. Knight and Alf Wilson were sitting directly ahead of Andrews. Wilson Brown, the second engineer, was alone in the seat behind Andrews. Johnnie dropped down beside him. Brown was a tall, slender man, with a thin, tense face, a shock of dark-brown hair, and an elegant, pointed mustache that drooped over the corners of his mouth. Like Knight, he was an experienced railroader, having served on the Mobile and Ohio. As Johnnie sat down, Brown nodded pleasantly.

"All aboard," sang the conductor. The cars jerked ahead with a clank of metal couplings, and the train pulled slowly away from the Marietta station. They were off! In a short time they would meet their first big test!

"Tickets please," said the conductor, moving down the aisle from the front of the coach. William Fuller was an amiable-looking young man of medium height, with friendly blue eyes, a trim mustache, and a funny little goatee. But despite his friendly manner and the little goatee, he looked shrewd, determined, and efficient. Johnnie noticed that, as Fuller took up tickets, he examined the passengers closely. "What's he looking for?" he whispered to Brown.

"Deserters, I guess," replied Brown. Johnnie

tried hard not to look like a deserter or a disguised Northern soldier as Fuller moved past him and on down the aisle. Andrews turned to Shadrack. "Did Hawkins and Porter make it?" he whispered. Shadrack shook his head.

Johnnie's excitement grew steadily. He was sitting over a flat wheel, and it seemed to him that the pounding of his heart kept time with the clanking of the wheel. He looked out the window, but he didn't really notice the scenery. In his mind's eye he was already at Big Shanty playing a heroic role in the theft of *The General*. His imagination leaped ahead and he was no longer Johnnie Adams, messenger boy, but Mr. John Adams, engineer. With Adams at the throttle, *The General* roared through Chattanooga and down the track to Bridgeport, where General Mitchel and his army hailed him as the hero of the hour. General Mitchel? Why not President Lincoln?

Suddenly Johnnie became aware that the train was slowing down. Could they be coming to Big Shanty? He looked at his watch. It was six o'clock. Yes, they were! Johnnie peered out the window. Nothing on that side. He looked across the aisle. His heart leaped. To the left of the train were parallel rows of tents, perpendicular to the track, extending into the woods beyond. Little groups of gray-clad soldiers were huddled over campfires cooking their breakfast. It was Camp McDonald! Johnnie gasped. For the first time the boldness of

Andrews' scheme struck Johnnie. How could they steal a train with thousands of Confederate soldiers looking on? He looked ahead where Andrews had been sitting. The seat was empty! Where could Andrews be? Had something gone wrong? His heart sank, but quickly rose again as Andrews strode calmly down the aisle. He smiled at Johnnie as he passed by to resume his seat. The man's quiet self-confidence reassured the young soldier.

The train slowed almost to a stop. On the right, a long, low shed, the building that gave the station its name, gradually came into view. Several passengers were waiting on the platform. The train hissed to a stop. "Big Shanty. Twenty minutes for breakfast," called Fuller. This was it, thought Johnnie.

Impulsively he started to rise, but Brown put out a restraining hand. On all sides passengers scrambled to their feet and crowded toward the front of the car. Andrews did not move. Johnnie looked out the window. At the far end of the platform he saw two of the train crew walking toward the station door. One he recognized as the engineer. If the other were the fireman, then the locomotive cab would be deserted. The coach was nearly empty now except for the raiders. Andrews rose. So did Knight. Andrews beckoned to Johnnie. Johnnie jumped to his feet and followed the two men down the aisle. Instead of descending

45

to the platform with the rest of the passengers, they got off on the opposite side, toward Camp McDonald. Johnnie's heart was pounding like a trip hammer, but Andrews seemed completely unconcerned. He led the way at a leisurely pace. No one paid any attention to them, neither the soldiers in the camp nor the sentries pacing up and down along the tracks. They were now abreast of the engine. A glance at the cab showed it to be empty! They walked a little way ahead of the engine. The track was clear. Without a word, Andrews turned and began to walk back at the same leisurely pace. The coolness of the man amazed Johnnie. Past the engine they went, past the tender, and finally past the three boxcars. As they reached the baggage car, Andrews turned to Knight. "Uncouple here," he said. Knight nodded, stepped between the boxcar and the baggage car, drew out the pin, and laid it carefully on the drawbar. Johnnie half expected Knight to be interrupted by a Confederate bayonet in the ribs, but still no one paid them any attention.

"Johnnie," said Andrews, "go get the others."

Johnnie mounted the steps of the coach, opened the door, stuck his head through the opening, and beckoned to Alf Wilson. The rest of the raiders were on their feet in an instant. They walked forward rapidly, but without pushing or shoving. Once on the ground, they dropped all pretense of casualness and dashed madly forward. Andrews was standing beside the open door of the rear box-car. It had not been open on their way back from the engine — Andrews must have opened it while Johnnie was giving the signal in the coach.

"In here, boys," said Andrews calmly.

The track was on an embankment so that the floor level of the car was breast-high from the ground. Andrews gave the first man, Pittenger, a boost into the car. Once in, Pittenger reached out to help the next man while those on the ground shoved him from behind. Ahead, Knight had already mounted to the cab. Andrews was walking forward with long, swift strides. Brown and Alf Wilson had detached themselves from the main group and were running at full speed toward the engine. Johnnie dashed after them. When he reached the cab, Andrews was standing with one foot on the bottom rung of the ladder and one hand on the handrail; he was facing toward the rear, watching the men clambering into the boxcar. Knight had cut the bell rope. His hand was on the throttle, his face tense, his eyes on Andrews. Wilson was gathering an armful of wood. Brown had his hand in the breast of his coat. Johnnie could see the butt of a pistol — Brown was ready to shoot if any of the sentries interfered. Johnnie scrambled to the top of the tender and looked back. He just couldn't believe his eyes. The whole affair was simply incredible. There, only ten feet away, stood a bored sentry watching the entire proceeding as if it were the most usual thing in the world for a group of disguised Yankees to steal a Confederate engine in plain view of thousands of Southerners. All but one of the raiders had climbed into the boxcar. As the last man — it was Ross — leaped aboard, he waved to Andrews. Andrews nodded to Knight and swung into the cab. Knight pulled back the throttle. With a hiss of steam, the giant wheels spun on the tracks, but Knight had opened the throttle too far and the train did not move. Then suddenly the wheels bit, and the engine leaped forward like a shot out of a cannon. Knight nearly bounced out of the engineer's seat, the other three older men crashed against the tender, and Johnnie fell flat on his back. When he picked himself up, Wilson was vigorously pounding Knight's shoulder; Brown was furiously pumping Andrews' hand. Johnnie's face lit up in a broad grin. They had done the impossible!

The train gathered speed and hurtled down the track. As they swept round the first curve, Johnnie looked back toward Big Shanty. Camp McDonald had sprung to life. Excited groups of soldiers gathered near the tracks. A few knelt, leveled their rifles, and fired at the rapidly fleeing train. Johnnie heard the shots and saw the puffs of smoke, but he knew they were already out of range. Across the tracks, the station was the scene of utter confusion. Frustrated passengers gazed in bewilderment at the marooned coaches and baggage car or ran confusedly about the platform, waving their arms and pointing at the disappearing *General*. Suddenly a single figure burst from the crowd and dashed madly down the track. It looked like Fuller. Johnnie laughed. You'll never catch us that way, he thought. In fact, there's no way at all you can catch us now.

The other occupants of the cab shared Johnnie's optimism. The usually calm Andrews made no attempt to conceal his joy. "Nice work, boys," he said, shaking hands with each man in turn.

Knight, his hand on the throttle, peered out the cab window at the track ahead. He grinned. "Stole a locomotive right out from under their noses. Easy as rolling off a log. Half the Confederate Army watching, too. We should have charged admission. Best show they'll ever see."

Brown checked the gauges and took his position at the opposite window from Knight, his mustache bristling more defiantly than ever. "They'll never stop us now," he said.

"No," agreed Andrews, who was leaning against the tender, "I don't think they will. Once we get past the local freight between here and Kingston, we should have clear sailing."

They had gone perhaps a mile and a half when a puzzled and worried look crept over Knight's face.

"What's the matter?" asked Andrews.

"Don't know. We're losing speed. Got the throttle wide open, too."

Brown rose from his seat by the window and peered at the steam gauge. "Steam pressure's falling. Almost none at all. Throw on some more wood, Alf."

"That's not the trouble," said Wilson. "I've fed her plenty of wood." He opened the door. The fire-box was crammed with billets, but the flames had dropped to a feeble flicker.

"Throw on some oil," directed Brown. Alf picked up the oilcan and squirted a few streams onto the fire. The flames sputtered weakly, but quickly died down again.

"What can be wrong?" asked Andrews.

Brown shook his head. "Blasted Confederate engine, that's what's the matter," growled Knight. "I knew these Southern railroads weren't any good. Nice shiny engine. Only trouble is it won't go."

The General had slowed almost to a stop and was puffing and wheezing like a fat man climbing a mountain. A few yards farther and the engine stopped dead on the tracks. Knight and Brown were visibly worried, but Andrews seemed unconcerned.

"Find out what's wrong and get her going again," he said to the two engineers. "Take your oilcan and oil her joints, Mr. Wilson. Up you go, Johnnie. Knock the insulators off and cut the wire." Andrews handed Johnnie a hammer and a small saw. Tucking these under his belt, Johnnie jumped to the ground and was up the pole like a cat. It was the work of only a minute to knock off the insulating box with the hammer and sever the tightly stretched wire with the saw.

From his perch atop the pole, Johnnie surveyed the scene below. Wilson was at the front of the engine, oiling the bearings in the journal boxes. Sleeves rolled up, the two engineers in the cab were feverishly trying to locate the trouble. Andrews had walked back to the boxcars to talk to the rest of the party. He looked as unconcerned as ever. The men in the boxcars had piled out to stretch their limbs. At a signal from Andrews, Ross had picked up the loose end of the wire Johnnie had cut and was tying it to an iron ring on the rear end of the first boxcar. When the train started up, the wire would be yanked loose.

Johnnie looked ahead of *The General*. To the north the track was clear for miles. He turned and looked in the other direction. From the top of the pole, Big Shanty was still within his range of vision. What he saw nearly made him fall from his perch. There a hundred yards or so from the depot, out of sight of the men on the ground but in plain view from the pole, was a squad of gray-clad soldiers marching down the track at double time.

"Mr. Andrews," he shouted, "they're after us. Around the bend. Double time. Thirty or forty of them!" Johnnie slid down the pole like a bolt of lightning and hit the ground with a thud that jarred him from head to foot. Slightly dazed, he staggered to his feet.

"Back into the cars, men," commanded Andrews, cool as ever, with only the slightest trace of excitement in his voice. "Stay there until I give the signal. Check your weapons. Have them ready for instant action!"

The men scrambled into the cars. Ross, as usual, was last, making sure that all was in order before he jumped in and closed the door.

Andrews took long strides toward the cab, Johnnie trotting after him. "Found the trouble?" Andrews asked.

"No," said Knight disgustedly, turning a soot-stained face streaked with oil and perspiration.

"Well, boys," said Andrews quietly, "you have about ten minutes to get this engine rolling, or it's all over with the Andrews raiders. Back at your post, Johnnie. Let me know when the enemy comes in sight." Johnnie clambered over the tender and onto the roof of the first boxcar. There he had an unobstructed view of the track. He shaded his eyes and peered anxiously at the curve in the roadbed.

"Say," said Brown, as if struck by a sudden inspiration, "maybe the Rebel engineer closed the draft when he stopped at Big Shanty."

"Right!" yelled Knight, springing into action and opening the dampers with a bang. "Come on, Alf! We'll have this buggy on the move in no time.

Soak some wood with oil. Make that fire roar! The boiler's still hot. We'll have steam up before you can say Jeff Davis. What a blockhead I am! Pour some oil on me and throw me in the firebox, too! I ought to have my head examined," Knight snorted.

"I don't take any prizes myself," muttered Brown.

Wilson saturated a pile of wood with oil. He opened the fire door and threw in all the box would take. The fire was already beginning to blaze furiously. Knight and Brown kept their eyes glued on the steam gauge. Johnnie kept his on the track. His heart was pounding as if it would burst through his ribs. Then it sank to the pit of his stomach. There they were! A gray-clad file burst into view, bayonets glistening in the sun. "Here they come!" Johnnie screamed.

5.
The General
Heads North

File after file swept round the bend. When they saw the stolen train stalled on the tracks, the Confederate soldiers shouted their triumphant yell and broke into a run. In the front line Johnnie saw Conductor Fuller do a little dance of delight at seeing his cherished *General*. Johnnie had never known a tenser moment. A matter of minutes, even seconds, would decide the fate of the raid. Andrews climbed up beside Johnnie and gazed steadily at their pursuers, not a sign of emotion showing in his face. Wilson's lips moved as if in prayer. Brown and Knight stared at the steam gauge with a pleading look in their eyes. "Come on, steam," Knight begged in a whisper. As though answering his plea, the needle quivered, hesitated, and then jumped ahead a hairsbreadth.

"She's coming," said Knight. "How much time do we have?"

"Maybe five minutes," answered Andrews. "They

can't run very fast with those heavy rifles, and they're still a mile away. That give you time enough?"

"I hope so," murmured Knight. "You give us a signal when you figure we can't delay any longer." Andrews nodded. "You better take her, Will," said Knight to Brown. "I've jinxed her so far."

Brown changed places with the other engineer. The needle on the steam gauge inched upward gradually but with infuriating slowness. Knight dug his fingernails into his palms. "Hurry, hurry," he said to himself.

On top of the boxcar, Johnnie and Andrews kept their eyes on the gray-clad soldiers. By now they had cut in half the distance between *The General* and the bend in the track. Fuller was still in front urging the soldiers to greater speed. It was a battle of time, distance, and nerves. Would the needle reach the critical point before the pursuers got to the train? Would Andrews have the nerve to delay the signal long enough? Johnnie looked at Andrews. His chin was set; a muscle quivered in his jaw. Johnnie was reassured. Andrews wouldn't fail them. If only *The General* came through, too. The soldiers kept advancing. Not so fast, pleaded Johnnie.

"How much time?" asked Brown.

"A minute or two," replied Andrews calmly.

"Ease her forward gently when the time comes, Will," cautioned Knight. "If you spin her the way I did back at Big Shanty, you'll shoot your wad and we'll be done for. Every ounce of steam counts." Brown nodded.

The needle kept rising slowly, steadily. But the Confederates kept coming, coming, coming. Five hundred yards, four hundred yards, three hundred yards. Andrews turned. "Can you do it now, boys?"

"I think so," replied Brown.

"Let 'er go, Will. Easy does it," said Knight.

Brown drew back the throttle bar delicately, gradually. There was a hiss of steam. Johnnie held his breath. The huge wheels turned slowly. *The General* shuddered, then moved forward. Knight opened the throttle a bit more. *The General* moved ahead a little faster. But the pursuers were still gaining. Two hundred yards. One hundred yards. Brown kept pulling the throttle bar back, gently but steadily. His nerves were as strong as Andrews — the temptation to throw the throttle wide open must have been almost irresistible. *The General* continued to gain momentum. The soldiers were shortening the gap much less rapidly. Seventy-five yards. For a few seconds the gap remained constant. Then *The General* began to gain, and the gray-clad soldiers began to fall back. All except Fuller. The gallant little conductor, running ahead of the soldiers and not encumbered with a rifle, had closed the gap to fifty yards. Andrews drew his pistol, cocked it, and leveled it at

Fuller. But before Andrews could pull the trigger, Fuller stumbled, turned a somersault, and fell in a heap on the roadbed. Johnnie heaved a sigh of relief — the pursuit was over!

Fuller jumped up and shook his fist at the train he had lost for the second time. The soldiers, coming up to the conductor, spread out across the track, knelt, aimed their rifles, and fired. "Get down, Johnnie," ordered Andrews. Johnnie jumped onto the tender and collapsed among the billets. Andrews leaped into the cab and mopped his forehead. Knight slumped in his seat. Wilson dropped his armful of oil-soaked wood and stood motionless in the center of the cab. Brown shook his head. "That was too close for comfort," he said.

Andrews slowly put his pistol in the inside pocket of his coat. "I didn't want to shoot Fuller," he said.

The noise of shots receded. A few bullets whistled harmlessly by. Then all was silent except for the welcome chugging of *The General* and the clatter of the wheels on the track.

"What was that fool Fuller doing chasing us on foot?" asked Brown.

"He must have figured us as deserters," answered Andrews. "Probably thought we'd abandon *The General* and flee into the woods."

Johnnie was again perched happily on the boxcar. The cool morning breeze fanned his forehead. Trees and telegraph poles rushed by. The wires rose and fell, rose and fell. The sky was overcast, but no rain had fallen yet. Johnnie peered at the roadbed. The track seemed clear. But was it? Johnnie narrowed his eyes. There was something ahead, far down the track. Johnnie thought he could distinguish human figures.

"Something on the track ahead," he called out. "Looks like a group of men."

"Probably a section gang," remarked Knight.

"Good. Perhaps we can 'borrow' some rail-lifting tools," said Andrews, smiling. "Get your pistols ready in case there's trouble." Brown put the throttle in neutral. Knight set the tender brakes. *The General* slowed rapidly. From his post on the boxcar, Johnnie could see a group of men beside the track leaning on their tools. As the train came to a halt, he noticed that the group consisted of a burly white foreman and four black laborers. The foreman looked puzzled as Andrews swung off and approached the group. "Good morning," he said to the foreman. "I'm running a special powder train to General Beauregard. Fuller gave us the right of way. He'll be along soon with his train." The puzzled look disappeared from the foreman's face. "We're short of tools. I'd like to borrow that crowbar," he said, pointing to a long pointed iron bar in the hand of one of the black workers.

"Yes, sir," replied the foreman in a heavy Irish brogue. He was obviously impressed by Andrews' distinguished appearance and quiet air of authority. In his frock coat and tall silk hat, Andrews looked the part of a trusted Southern gentleman placed in charge of an important mission. "Hand it over, Tom," the foreman said to the laborer. The black man did as he was told.

"Thank you, sir," said Andrews, taking the crowbar. "General Beauregard will be grateful." With a courtly wave Andrews turned, walked to the cab, and handed the newly acquired tool to Knight. Knight accepted the bar absentmindedly — he seemed concerned about something.

"How about that?" he asked, pointing at a handcar which lay beside the track a few feet ahead of the engine. Johnnie hadn't noticed it; neither apparently had Andrews. Andrews looked at the handcar and shook his head. He climbed into the cab. "Roll her," he said to Brown.

Brown pulled back the throttle. *The General* moved ponderously forward. Andrews turned to Knight, whose face still showed his concern over the handcar.

"Don't worry about it, Mr. Knight," said Andrews. "No one can catch us in a handcar. And it's important not to arouse any suspicion as we go along."

Knight shifted his concern to the crowbar in his hand. "This blasted thing won't help us much. We should have a bar with a claw on the end."

"Well, it's the best they had." Andrews turned

to Brown. "As soon as we're out of sight of the section gang, we better stop to lift a rail. That will fix your handcar for you," Andrews said with a smile at Knight. A sharp curve loomed ahead. "Stop on the other side of the bend," ordered Andrews. Knight set the brakes. *The General* took the curve easily, and gradually came to a halt. Andrews addressed Knight. "Make a careful inspection of the engine. Oil her thoroughly. Be sure everything's in order for a long run." Then, turning to Wilson and handing him a red flag that Brown had found in a corner of the cab, "Hang this on the back of the last boxcar. The flag will support our story that Fuller is behind us with his mail train. Johnnie, up you go again."

Andrews alighted from the cab and strode back to the first boxcar, carrying the crowbar in his hand. Wilson followed with the red flag. Armed with the oilcan, Knight made his way toward the front of the locomotive. Tucking his hammer and saw into his belt, Johnnie jumped to the ground, ran to the nearest pole, and shinnied to the top. There, in a minute's time, he had smashed the insulator and sawed through the wire. Down below, Knight was oiling the journals at one end of the train and Wilson was setting the flag in a bracket at the other end. Andrews had opened the door of the first boxcar, and the men were spilling out and down the embankment. Johnnie saw Andrews lay a restraining hand on George Wilson as he was about to jump. Wilson disappeared into the car and reappeared almost immediately carrying two axes. Leaping to the ground, he gave one of the axes to Perry Shadrack. The two axmen walked rapidly to the first pole beyond the end of the train. Stripping off their coats and rolling up their shirt sleeves, they attacked the pole with rhythmic alternating blows. Chips of wood flew in all directions.

Andrews handed the iron bar to Ross. The rest of the men followed the Sergeant past the boxcars and beyond the pole where George Wilson and Shadrack were vigorously wielding their axes. Where two sections of iron rail joined over a wooden tie, Ross applied the crowbar to the spikes which fastened the rail to the tie. Pittenger led a small group to a pile of sleepers lying at the bottom of the embankment. Each man picked up a sleeper and carried it with him to the track where Ross was working. Wonder what they want those for, thought Johnnie. Ross was having his troubles with the spikes. "This blasted bar is no good," he growled. "We need a claw to draw out the spikes."

"I know," remarked Andrews, "but it's the best we have."

Alternately prying and pounding, Ross managed to loosen one or two spikes. Then he inserted the point of his bar between the rail and the tie. Pittenger placed his sleeper alongside the track. Using this as a fulcrum, Ross pushed down on his bar. Beads of sweat rolled off his forehead; his face grew red with effort; the veins in his neck stood out; muscles bulged in his forearms. Slowly the rail rose. "I've got it," grunted Ross. As soon as there was space enough, Pittenger inserted a new sleeper under the rail beside the crowbar. Ross withdrew his bar and went to work on the spikes joining the rail to the next tie. In this way he worked gradually toward the point where the rail section ended and a new one began. Soon the entire length of the rail section was lined with men pushing and straining with their sleepers. "She's coming, boys," muttered Ross. "Once more! Heave!" Then with a sharp snap the rail broke loose. The sudden release sent the men tumbling in all directions. As they picked themselves up and dusted off their shirts and trousers, Shadrack sang out, "Timber!" The pole fell across the tracks with a loud crash, ripping wires from the poles on either side.

"What'll we do with the rail, Mr. Andrews?" asked Ross.

"Take it along with us," replied Andrews. Ross, Pittenger, and Shadrack lifted the rail. "The rest of you carry sleepers. They may be useful later." Each of the soldiers shouldered a sleeper. When the end boxcar was reached, rail and ties were thrown in. The men climbed into the first car. "We're coming to Acworth, boys," warned Andrews. "Keep concealed. This won't look much like a powder train if you show your faces." Looking up at Johnnie, he asked, "How's the track, Johnnie?"

"All clear both ways," replied Johnnie. He slid to the ground and ran to the cab. Alf Wilson had the fire door open and was throwing a fresh pile of wood on the roaring flames. Knight had released the brakes; Brown's hand was on the throttle, ready for the signal.

"Let her go, Mr. Brown," said Andrews. He looked at his watch. "We're a little behind schedule. Run her up to twenty miles per hour, but slow down for the stations."

"I've checked *The General* thoroughly, Mr. Andrews," reported Knight. "She's in perfect running order."

"Enough water?"

"Enough for a while."

"How about the wood, Mr. Wilson?"

Alf nodded.

Andrews rubbed his hands; he was obviously pleased. "Everything is going fine, boys. We've now blocked all pursuit from behind. No locomotive from Atlanta will be able to get past the break in the track. We're safe as far as Kingston. And when we get beyond Kingston, we'll lift another rail to prevent pursuit from there. Even Knight's handcar won't be able to catch us." Knight grinned at Andrews' joke. "And with the wires down, the Confederates won't even be able to send a message ahead."

"They can't anyway, with no telegraph office at Big Shanty," remarked Knight.

"I'm just making doubly sure," countered Andrews. "Someone might have a portable transmitter. And I want to be certain that no message gets through from the other side of Big Shanty in case Fuller sends a messager back toward Atlanta."

Rain was beginning to fall in a light drizzle, making Johnnie's post on the catwalk somewhat damp and cool. But not enough so to drive him down into the cab. As far as he was concerned, he had the post of honor, and it would take more than a little rain to force him to surrender it. He was the eyes of the expedition, and he enjoyed being the first to see what lay ahead. He also liked the feel of the wind rushing past and the rain beating in his face. He wouldn't have exchanged places with anyone in the world.

Soon, scattered houses began to dot the countryside. "Looks like a town ahead," he called out.

"Acworth," said Andrews. "Slow her down, Mr. Brown. Go through the town at half speed."

Brown shoved the throttle into the neutral position. *The General* gradually slowed to eight miles an hour. As the train approached the town, Johnnie could see the passengers emerge from the depot and take places on the platform ready to board the train. You're in for a surprise, my good fellows, he thought, chuckling. As *The General* steamed past the station, Johnnie saw the looks of astonishment and disappointment on the faces of the passengers. One or two late arrivals dashed from the waiting room with carpetbags flapping in their hands, and stood openmouthed as the train gave no sign of stopping. The shirt-sleeved stationmaster, a pencil perched behind his ear and a visor projecting from his forehead, scratched his head in bewilderment.

"Mail will be along in a little while," sang out Andrews, leaning out over the platform. Johnnie waved gaily at the passengers.

"Maybe that and the red will satisfy the stationmaster," Andrews said. "At least until we cut the wires again. Stop around the next curve, Mr. Brown. Ready, Johnnie?" Johnnie nodded, jumped down onto the tender, stumbled over the woodpile and into the cab, and stuck the saw and hammer in his belt. As *The General* wheezed to a stop at the end of a long curve, Johnnie was on the embankment and up the pole in a flash. When the severed wire dropped to the ground, Knight picked it up and tied it to a ringbolt on the last boxcar. It was only a matter of minutes before Johnnie and Knight were back in the cab and *The General* was chugging ahead once more. Johnnie looked at his watch. It was 7:10.

Fifteen minutes later they passed through Allatoona. This is where I get off, thought Johnnie, smiling as he remembered the ticket he had bought back at Marietta; got to see my sick grandmother. Again he waved at the disappointed passengers and the puzzled stationmaster, and again Andrews called out his assurance that the mail would be along soon. As he turned to watch the station recede in the distance, Johnnie saw the length of telegraph wire dancing merrily along behind the train. Hope nobody noticed it, he thought. When they were out of sight of Allatoona, they stopped again to cut wire. This time Andrews let the men out of the boxcar to stretch their limbs and sent George Wilson back with his ax to sever the length of wire tied to the boxcar outside Acworth. One dancing wire would be less noticeable than two.

Back in the cab and under way again, the train thieves were jubilant. Andrews rubbed his hands in his characteristic gesture of satisfaction. "You're doing nobly, boys," he said. "Everything's working perfectly."

"Just like taking candy from a baby," remarked Knight.

"Yeah, but let's hope the baby doesn't tell his mother," growled Wilson with his usual pessimism.

"What's the matter with you, Alf?" asked Knight disgustedly.

"Nuthin', I'm just ready for anything. Somethin's bound to happen. It can't be this easy."

"Nothing can go wrong, Mr. Wilson," said Andrews confidently. "With no engines between Atlanta and Kingston, how can they chase us, let alone catch us? We'll be at Kingston within two hours. There we'll let the southbound freight pass us. And when we get outside Kingston we'll pull up a rail and immobilize the engines at Kingston. We can't fail. The hardest part is over."

"Two hours to Kingston? That's only ten miles an hour. Can't we go any faster?" asked Brown.

"Not if we keep to Fuller's schedule. Following his schedule will make it easier for us to get by the southbound trains."

"We ought to sell *The General* and buy a horse," Knight muttered contemptuously. "These Southern railroads have the speed of an old woman on crutches."

"It's a hilly, winding road. And the rails are worn thin with the heavy war traffic. It would be dangerous to go very fast."

Johnnie was back on the catwalk. He shared the good spirits of the men in the cab. He twirled his cap on his forefinger and whistled "Dixie." "After all, I'm supposed to be a Southerner," he said to himself. Suddenly his attention was caught by a pillar of black smoke rising into the air ahead of the train and slightly to the right.

"Smoke ahead," he called out.

"Probably from the Etowah Ironworks. About five miles west of the track," replied Andrews.

Johnnie kept his eyes on the black cloud. It grew larger and larger. But it remained almost straight ahead. Johnnie was puzzled. If it were from the ironworks, it should gradually veer westward as the train came nearer. But it didn't. It kept growing blacker and larger and stayed in front of *The General*. The locomotive thundered across a long bridge high over a river. Hope *The General* doesn't crave a swim, thought Johnnie, looking fearfully at the water far below.

Off to the right Johnnie saw a single track winding down the hills toward the main line. Probably a spur running up to the ironworks, he guessed. He followed the course of the spur as it gradually worked its way toward the Western and Atlantic track. He looked ahead to see if he could discover where the two tracks met. Yes, there was the junction, right where the black cloud seemed to originate. Johnnie narrowed his eyes. Suddenly, he realized what was causing the smoke. There on the spur, clouds billowing from its stack, stood a locomotive, fired up and ready to move! And Andrews said there were no engines between Atlanta and Kingston!

6.
The Red Flag

L ocomotive ahead!" Johnnie yelled.

"What!" exploded Andrews, placing one hand on the handrail and swinging out over the embankment. For the first time since Johnnie had known him, the agent's composure was ruffled.

"Yep, there she is," said Brown. Wilson and Knight crowded Brown's window to get a look at the unexpected enemy.

Andrews withdrew into the cab. "I've been over this road four or five times and I've never seen this engine before. Must belong to the ironworks."

"Whoever it belongs to, we better get rid of it," said Knight emphatically.

Andrews' brow furrowed. He hesitated, then shook his head. "No," he said, "it won't make any difference."

"Won't make any difference!" Knight's countenance was purple. "It just gives the Johnny Rebs a pursuing locomotive right on our tail, instead of forty-five miles back in Atlanta, that's all." An-

69

drews said nothing. Knight continued, "We can overpower the engineer and fireman and smash that wagon so it won't run for weeks. Then we can burn that big bridge behind us."

The General was now passing over the switch where the spur joined the Western and Atlantic track. Down the spur a short way was a turntable where the ironworks engine could be faced in either direction. The engine itself was now directly opposite *The General* at a point where the spur paralleled the main line. The word "Yonah" printed on the boiler was plainly visible to the Union soldiers. *The Yonah* was older and smaller than *The General,* but it looked sturdy and powerful and would obviously give the Confederates an effective instrument of pursuit. The engineer and the fireman were in the cab; a small group of men stood beside the locomotive. They looked dubiously at *The General.* Andrews waved; they waved back.

The Yonah gradually receded from sight as Brown opened *The General*'s throttle. Andrews turned toward Knight, who was sputtering angrily and unintelligibly. "I understand your feeling, Mr. Knight. We could probably burn the bridge. But we would gain nothing that we have not already gained by lifting that rail behind us. We're burning bridges to help General Mitchel; burning a bridge here won't accomplish that. All we would do is arouse the countryside.

"As for *The Yonah*, we could destroy her all right. And I guess we could overcome those men back there. But suppose just one should get away. Or suppose, while we lose a valuable twenty minutes here, the southbound freight should come in sight. It could ram us and wreck us, it could raise a barricade in our way, or it could run back to Kingston and give the alarm. Then the Confederates would have us boxed in between Kingston and Big Shanty. The longer we can conceal our identity and our purpose, the better our chances of success. We don't want the alarm raised here. As long as Big Shanty is the closest point where we have tipped our hand, we're safe."

Andrews' quietly convincing tone and the logic of his argument had its effect on Knight as it always did on everyone who heard Andrews talk. "Maybe you're right," agreed Knight. "Anyway, you're the boss."

"*The Yonah* looks as if she's ready to set out for the ironworks anyhow," remarked Brown. "She can't do us any harm up there."

Ten minutes later they passed through Cartersville. Again Johnnie was amused at the puzzled bewilderment and pained disappointment of the passengers on the platform. As soon as the station was out of sight, Andrews signaled a halt. Quick as a flash Johnnie was up and the line was down. The men tumbled out of the boxcar. Ross attached the severed wire to a cleat beneath the boxcar door.

The men scrambled back, *The General* chugged ahead, and the wire jerked loose. This time George Wilson leaned out and cut the wire from the cleat with his ax. Now there was no dancing snake to catch suspicious eyes.

"Wood's getting low, Mr. Andrews," reported Wilson.

"So's the water," said Knight, peering at the water gauge.

"We'll stop at Cass, then," said Andrews. "It's a wood and water station."

The run to Cass was accomplished without incident. From his post atop the boxcar Johnnie was the first to sight the station, a small, low, dingy-looking shed. Beyond it rose the water tank perched precariously on four spindly legs, the water spout rising in an arc from the base of the tank. Beside the tank, firewood lay stacked in neatly piled tiers. Brown eased *The General* up to the tank and stopped the tender directly beneath the spout. Knight leaped out of the cab, climbed the ladder to the narrow platform encircling the tank, and swung the hose out over the tender. Johnnie lifted the hinged manhole cover in *The General*'s tender, drew down the hose, and plunged it into the opening. Propelled by the force of gravity, the water rushed through the hose and into the tank. Knight descended the ladder and Johnnie jumped to the ground. Stationing themselves by the woodpile, they took turns passing wood to Alf Wilson, who was standing by the wood box in the forward section of the tender.

The door to the depot opened with a clatter. A short, powerfully built man in overalls strode angrily toward *The General*. Knight looked up. "Here comes the yard foreman," he warned Andrews. Andrews walked to meet the Confederate railroad man.

"Where's Fuller and the regular crew?" the foreman demanded loudly. He looked both belligerent and suspicious. "Where's the rest of the mail train? What're you doing with *The General?*"

"Fuller will be along shortly," replied Andrews calmly. "I'm running a powder special to General Beauregard at Corinth. Fuller gave me *The General* and the three boxcars of the early mail." Andrews was at his dignified and authoritative best. As usual, his manner and appearance won immediate belief.

"Sorry, sir," said the foreman respectfully. "I'll help with the wood."

"Never mind that. Can you give me a timetable? Those fools in Atlanta sent me roaring down the track with three carloads of powder and no table to run by. Never occurred to them that I'd have to know the schedules of the southbound trains."

The foreman shuddered as he pictured the result of a collision. "Yes, sir, I'll get mine," he said, running toward the depot with surprising agility for one of his build. In a moment, he was back, proudly waving a timetable. "Here, sir," he said.

"Sorry to take your only table," Andrews apologized.

"I'd send my only shirt to General Beauregard if he needed it," replied the foreman.

"I'll see that the authorities hear of your cooperation," said Andrews.

The foreman swelled with pride. Without another word, he joined Johnnie and Knight at the woodpile. In a few minutes' time, the wood box was full. Johnnie climbed to the tender to check the tank. "Nearly full, sir," he reported to Andrews.

"That's good enough," said Andrews. "We can't keep General Beauregard waiting."

Johnnie removed the hose and let it swing back and up to its original arc above the water tank. Andrews and Knight climbed into the cab. Brown opened the throttle and *The General* hissed laboriously forward. "Much obliged," Andrews called to the foreman, who was ascending the ladder to secure the hose.

"Yes, sir," he said and waved at the departing powder train.

"This table's a gold mine," remarked Andrews. "Now we'll know exactly where and when to pass the southbound trains. Boys, this raid is going to work. We'll join General Mitchel tonight or my name's not James Andrews."

"You bet we will," shouted Johnnie with boyish enthusiasm. He grinned sheepishly.

"That's the spirit, Johnnie," said Andrews. He pulled out his watch, then consulted the timetable. "Eight-forty. We're running on schedule. Due in Kingston at nine-eleven. Southbound freight should be waiting for us. Nonstop to Kingston, boys."

"How about the wires?" asked Knight.

"We don't have to worry about that between here and Kingston. There was no telegraph at Cass." Andrews removed his silk hat and donned a railroad cap which he pulled from his pocket. From another pocket he extracted a long black cigar, bit off the end, stuck the cigar between his teeth at a jaunty angle, applied a light, and blew huge clouds of smoke contentedly into the air. The transformation was complete: James J. Andrews, respected Confederate official, had given way to James J. Andrews, Federal train thief.

But when, thirty minutes later, *The General* slowed for the Kingston yards, the cap had disappeared and the silk hat had taken its place. Despite Andrews' confidence and his elation at getting a timetable, everyone sensed that a crucial moment, perhaps the most crucial of the entire raid, had arrived. Kingston was the largest town through which they had yet passed. Furthermore, it was a railroad junction. There would be switches to pass over. Inquisitive switch tenders and perhaps even engineers, conductors, and brakemen might ask pointed and embarrassing questions that would have to be answered. If the stolen train had to wait for the down freight, there would be hordes of angry passengers to contend with; perhaps among them would be an important Confederate official who might see through Andrews' powder story and even doubt the validity of the signed order from General Beauregard. Then there were the stationmaster, the baggage agent, and the telegraph operator, whose suspicions might have to be lulled. If only the freight were waiting on the side track and they could rush through Kingston without stopping. Once beyond Kingston, they could cut wire and tear up track, thus blocking pursuit even if Confederate suspicions were aroused. The danger lay in being suspected while *The General* was immobilized by the approaching freight. If that happened, then the stolen train would never leave Kingston in Yankee hands. The thought of discovery and capture, followed by imprisonment and execution, sent a shiver down Johnnie's spine.

Johnnie peered ahead. The Kingston station, its platform crowded with passengers awaiting Fuller's train, lay to the left of the track. Still farther to the left was the siding, which joined the main line at the end of the depot platform. But the siding was empty! The freight had not yet arrived. They would have to wait and brazen it out as best they could. Beyond the siding and parallel to it ran the spur from Rome; this too joined the main line a few hundred yards ahead. Standing on the spur was the Rome local, three cars and an engine.

"Freight here, Johnnie?" asked Andrews.

"No, sir. The siding's empty."

Andrews shook his head. "Too bad. Well, it can't be helped. Pull her past the switch, Mr. Brown, then back her in. I'll drop off at the station and get the switch tender."

"There's a passenger train on another track, Mr. Andrews," said Johnnie.

"That's the Rome local. She won't cause us any trouble. Just runs back and forth between Kingston and Rome. She's waiting for Fuller's mail," explained Andrews.

The General moved slowly toward the station. Passengers on the platform picked up their luggage; others emerged through the waiting-room door. The telegraph operator banged his window shut and a few seconds later appeared beside the track, a piece of paper fluttering in his right hand. The baggage master trundled his trunk toward the far end of the platform. As *The General* drew opposite the depot, Andrews swung off and pushed his way through the crowd toward the stationmaster's office. The telegraph operator trailed after him insistently waving his piece of paper. Brown eased the train over the switch. Johnnie looked back toward the station. A side door opened with a loud clatter and out shot a tattered figure. Andrews strode angrily through the door. The tattered man stumbled to a halt and waved his hands excitedly — in one of them dangled a huge bunch of keys. Must be the switch tender, thought Johnnie. Andrews pushed the switchman toward the stolen train. Johnnie could hear their heated voices. "But I don't have no orders about no special train."

"Listen, my good man," said Andrews with exaggerated patience, "I have three boxcars of highly explosive powder. If you wish to take the responsibility of leaving those cars on the main track in the way of the down freight, you may do so. Perhaps you'd like to explain to General Beauregard why his powder never reached him, and tell Governor Brown how the whole town of Kingston happened to be blown to bits."

This brought the old man to his senses. Grumbling and muttering to himself, he shuffled to the junction, inserted a key in the lock, and laboriously closed the switch so that the stolen train could back in. Andrews signaled to Brown. The engineer threw *The General* in reverse. The boxcars moved slowly over the switch and down the siding. As the locomotive passed the junction, the old man opened the switch again and turned the key in the lock. Andrews walked up to the cab. "Keep an eye on that fellow, Mr. Knight. That key of his can hold us on this siding for the rest of the day. Where's that blasted freight?" he asked irritably.

"It's late, sir," said the telegraph operator, who had followed Andrews out of the depot. "Here's a telegram for Fuller ordering him to wait here. I suppose you should have it." Andrews read the order and returned it to the operator. "Too bad to keep you here," said the telegrapher. "Maybe I should wire Adairsville to hold the freight."

"Too late," said Andrews quickly. "It's already left Adairsville." Johnnie shuddered. A message ahead! Nothing could be more dangerous.

"Wonder why Atlanta didn't tell us about your powder train," continued the operator. Why doesn't this guy keep his mouth shut, thought Johnnie.

"I can't understand it," replied Andrews with feigned indignance. He paced nervously back and forth beside *The General*.

Ten minutes later the welcome sound of a whistle rent the air. "Here she comes," said Andrews with no attempt to conceal his relief. "Everything ready?"

"Yes, sir," answered Brown. "She's all oiled and rarin' to go." Turning to Knight, "You take her from here, Bill."

"Right, Will," said Knight, shifting to the engineer's seat.

The southbound freight chugged around the

bend and headed slowly down the straightaway. As the engine, pulling a string of boxcars, passed over the switch, the stationmaster appeared on the platform and waved the freight down the track so as to clear the way for *The General*. One by one the cars clattered past the junction. Brown released the tender brake; Knight put his hand on the throttle. As the last car crossed the switch, a startled exclamation broke from Knight. "Look," he said, pointing to the end of the freight. Andrews' face went pale. Johnnie looked in the direction Knight was pointing. A red flag! Another train was following close behind! *The General* could not leave Kingston!

7.
A Whistle
from the South

The conductor of the freight had jumped to the platform. Andrews ran to intercept him — Johnnie had never seen the Federal agent move so rapidly. "Conductor," Andrews shouted commandingly. The conductor stopped. "What's the red flag for?"

"Extra train."

"Extra? What do you mean?"

"Yanks are threatening Chattanooga. The authorities ordered all rolling stock south. Made up a special in the Chattanooga yards. Can't let the Federals capture our cars — we've few enough already."

"But I'm running a powder special to General Beauregard. Blast those people at Atlanta! If they want Beauregard to get his powder, they should give me a clear track. Powder's more important than boxcars. How far behind is the extra?"

"Dunno. Mebbe ten or fifteen minutes."

"Well, there's nothing to do but wait," said Andrews wearily. "You'll have to move down the track a bit so the extra can clear the switch for my train."

"I'll be pulling out for Atlanta in a minute or two, soon's I check with the stationmaster."

"If you do, you'll run smack into Fuller's mail. I'm carrying a red flag, too," said Andrews, pointing to the stolen train.

"Oh! I guess we're both stuck here. Well, I'm in no hurry."

"I am, blast it!"

"Where you taking the powder?"

"Corinth."

"Corinth! You'll never make it. General Mitchel's captured Huntsville."

"I don't believe it. Mitchel wouldn't dare move so deep into our territory."

"But he has. Yesterday morning's express rolled through Huntsville just as Mitchel arrived. Yanks opened fire, but the express got away. Hasn't been a blasted train from the west since."

"Well, Beauregard will see that Mitchel doesn't stay there long. Anyway, I have my orders."

"Orders or no orders, you won't get through." The conductor disappeared into the depot. Andrews turned and walked toward the stolen train.

"Johnnie!" he called. Johnnie leaped from the tender and ran up to Andrews.

"Tell the men in the cab we've got to wait for an extra," Andrews said in a low voice. "Then pass the word to the boxcar boys. Take a hammer and bang on the rods underneath the car while you're talking. Don't let anyone suspect what you're up to. I'm going to keep an eye on the telegraph operator. We can't let him send any messages north while we're stranded here."

"Yes, sir." As Andrews made his way to the telegraph office, Johnnie walked to the cab.

"What's up, Johnnie?" asked Knight.

"Got to wait for an extra."

"I thought so. Old Stars was right. A day's delay and we'd find the track crowded with refugee trains."

"Easy as pie. Nothing can stop us now," mocked Alf Wilson maliciously.

"Ah, shut up, Alf," growled Knight.

Wilson grinned.

"How you getting along with the switchman?" asked Johnnie.

"Well, I'm not having any trouble keeping him in sight. He's buzzing around like an angry fly."

"He likes you," grinned Alf.

"What a pest," grumbled Knight. "He asks more questions than a three-year-old."

Johnnie grabbed a hammer from the box under the engineer's seat and walked back to the door of the first car. Reaching under the car, he began tapping one of the rods, keeping his face close to the door. "Can you hear me? It's Johnnie." Johnnie caught a muffled reply. "We can't leave yet. Have to wait for an extra. Old Stars has the Southerners in a panic. They're clearing all their stock out of Chattanooga. Everything's okay. We'll be off soon."

Johnnie straightened up, returned the hammer to the cab, and went off to report to Andrews. The Union spy was in the telegraph office. "Delivered your message, Mr. Andrews," Johnnie said.

"Good boy, Johnnie."

Andrews was leaning casually over the back of a chair, one foot resting on the bottom rung. He looked as if he hadn't a worry in the world. But Johnnie noticed that his right hand was thrust purposefully beneath the bosom of his coat. One false move and the telegrapher would be looking into the barrel of a pistol. Outside, the drizzle had increased to a downpour. The platform was deserted. Fine weather for bridge burning, Johnnie thought. He looked at the huge clock on the wall. 9:45. They had been delayed at Kingston for nearly thirty-five minutes. By now they should have been in Adairsville.

"Where's that extra?" muttered Andrews. "Any word from Adairsville?"

"No, sir," answered the operator. "Want me to contact them?"

"Don't bother. It won't do any good. I've just got to wait, that's all."

The big clock ticked the seconds away with agonizing slowness. Every swing of the gold pendulum increased the chances of pursuit from the south and decreased the chances of a successful run north. Johnnie had never known time to drag so. 9:50 ... 9:55 ... 10:00 ... Andrews shifted his weight uneasily. Then, the sound of a whistle from the north.

"Here she comes, sir," said the telegrapher.

Andrews bounded from the room. Johnnie followed as Andrews raced down the siding toward *The General.* "Get set, boys," Andrews called out. Knight took the engineer's seat. Wilson threw a fresh load of wood into the firebox. Andrews turned to the switch tender. "Close that switch as soon as the extra passes the junction."

"Yes, sir," said the old man, shuffling toward the main line.

"Another red flag and I'll throw myself under the wheels of *The General,*" remarked Brown.

The southbound locomotive rumbled slowly over the switch. The conductor dropped off and walked toward *The General.* One by one the cars clattered past the junction as the extra steadily lost speed. The brakeman atop the boxcars spun their wheels. As the train shuddered to a halt, a string of flatcars extended beyond the switch and down the track in the direction of Adairsville.

Andrews met the conductor of the extra halfway between the siding and the main track. "You'll have to clear the switch, sir," he said. "I'm running powder to General Beauregard, and I'm already well behind schedule."

"Glad to, but you can't leave the siding now."

"Why not?" barked Andrews.

"Track's not clear ahead," the conductor replied, pointing to the last car on the extra. As if in answer to the conductor, a gust of wind sprang up. A flag at the end of the train flapped in the breeze. It was red! Johnnie's knees went weak. Andrews' shoulders sagged. Wilson slammed a billet to the floor in disgust. Knight leaned disconsolately on the throttle.

"Well, I'll be boiled in oil," muttered Brown.

Andrews recovered his composure. "What's the meaning of this?" he asked in a level tone.

"Too many cars for one engine," was the answer. "Had to split the extra. Second section's up the track somewhere."

For once Andrews was too crushed to protest. He walked wearily toward the depot. Johnnie tagged along behind — he might be needed as a messenger boy. This time the telegrapher had company: the stationmaster, the engineer of the Rome train, and the conductor of the regular freight.

"Mighty funny that we've had no instructions from Atlanta 'bout a powder train," the stationmaster was saying. As Andrews entered the office, the group eyed him suspiciously.

But Andrews was undisturbed. "If you gentlemen have any doubts about me or my train, here is an order signed by General Beauregard." Andrews reached into his pocket, pulled out an official-looking document, and handed it to the stationmaster. The stationmaster looked it over carefully, then returned it to Andrews.

"Beg your pardon, sir. No offense meant."

"That's all right. I don't wonder you're concerned. Can't understand why Atlanta didn't notify you."

The stationmaster turned to the operator. "When did you hear from Atlanta last?"

"Over four hours ago."

"See if you can get them." Johnnie tensed, but Andrews gave no sign of alarm. The telegrapher tapped his key; a look of concern spread over his face.

"Can't get through. Line's gone dead."

Andrews spoke up quickly. "That explains why you haven't heard from Atlanta. They surely must have tried to notify you about the powder train."

"Is the line open to the north?"

The operator tapped his key again. Within a minute or two, an answer clicked on the receiver set. "Line's clear to Adairsville. Second section of the extra went through twenty minutes ago."

"Where's Fuller?" demanded the conductor of the regular freight.

"That's what I'd like to know," broke in the

Rome engineer. "He's way overdue. I can't wait here forever."

"Perhaps I ought to move my train on toward Atlanta and find out what's the matter," suggested the conductor.

"You can't do that," said Andrews. "Fuller's blocking your way. Stop worrying, he'll be along soon." Andrews opened the door and beckoned Johnnie to follow. Out on the platform, the rain fell in torrents. "You'd better warn the boys that there may be trouble. Tell them to be ready for anything. We may have to shoot it out or break for the hills to the west. These Kingston people are getting suspicious."

As Johnnie turned to go, the door opened; the three Confederate railroad men appeared and walked toward the waiting-room door. Johnnie breathed a sigh of relief — now Andrews could handle the telegrapher more easily. Johnnie pulled his cap down, turned up his collar, and hunched his shoulders against the rain. Since the yard was entirely deserted, Johnnie didn't bother with the hammer ruse but walked directly to the boxcar. He opened the door slightly.

"This is Johnnie again. We're waiting for the second section of the extra. The railroad people here are getting pretty fidgety. Andrews says be ready for a scrap or a flight to the hills."

"Okay, Johnnie." It was Ross's voice.

In the cab, Knight was still having his troubles with the switch tender. As Johnnie walked up, the old man descended from the cab, where he had sought refuge from the downpour, and shuffled toward the depot. Knight followed.

"Good riddance," muttered Brown. "That old guy is a walking encyclopedia of Southern railroads. Knows everybody but us. Thinks we're phonies."

"The men at the depot are getting suspicious, too. Andrews is afraid there may be trouble. He says to be ready to fight or run for our lives."

"Look at the snarl these tracks are in," continued Brown. "Four trains here already and a fifth on the way. We'll be lucky to get out of here alive."

"The day's delay will ruin us yet," observed Wilson. "Yesterday we'd've had a clear track and a clear day. How can we burn bridges in this rain?"

Brown ignored Alf's question. "We should have moved out after the regular freight arrived. By running at full speed, we could have reached Adairsville before the extra left there."

"Except that Andrews didn't know the extra would take so long to get here. And he didn't know the extra would be in two sections," Johnnie said in defense of Andrews.

Johnnie hurried back to the telegraph office. Knight and the switchman were there, too. As Johnnie entered, Andrews ordered Knight back to the engine. Johnnie looked at the clock. 10:15. They had been at Kingston a full hour. If we don't get away soon, our goose is cooked, thought Johnnie. As if in answer to this unspoken plea, the stillness was shattered by the screech of a whistle.

Andrews moved into action at once. "I want that switch adjusted for my train as soon as the extra clears the junction." The switchman didn't budge. "Did you hear what I said?" asked Andrews sharply.

"I heard you," was the surly reply. "But I ain't taking down my keys until I know by what authority you're ordering everybody around."

Johnnie's mouth dropped, but Andrews only laughed. "I can't waste my time on you." He strode to the wall where the switchman's keys hung on a hook, took them down, and tossed them to Johnnie. "Tell Brown to tend the switch." Andrews moved through the door, followed by Johnnie and the sputtering switchman.

"I'll report you to the authorities. I'll have you locked up for this."

The stationmaster was already on the platform. "Be sure the extra clears the switch," said Andrews.

The stationmaster looked up in surprise. "You can't leave now. You won't be able to get through Adairsville. There's a down freight on the siding there now waiting for the southbound passenger from Dalton. If it's on time, the passenger will be en route here before you reach Adairsville."

"I can't delay any longer. Beauregard has got to have his powder. I'll have to take the risk."

Johnnie flew over the distance between the depot and *The General*. The switch tender hobbled after him. Johnnie tossed the keys to Brown. "Old man Methuselah got stubborn. You'll have to tend the switch." Brown caught the keys and moved toward the switch, followed by the irate Southern railroader. As the freight rumbled over the switch, Brown inserted his key. The stationmaster waved the extra down the track. Johnnie climbed to his perch on the boxcar. Knight fingered the throttle. Andrews stood with one foot on the ladder and one hand on the handrail. When the last car clattered by, Brown pushed against the switch lever. The switch clicked into place. *The General* rolled forward. As it swung onto the main line, Brown tossed the keys to the switchman and jumped aboard. The old man shook his fist.

Andrews removed his hat and mopped his brow with a silk handkerchief. "What an ordeal." He looked at his watch. "Ten-twenty. We've lost an hour and five minutes. I hate to stop again but we've got to cut the wires. Brake her around the first bend, Mr. Knight."

Once around the bend, Knight threw *The General* into reverse and Brown applied the tender brake. "Hurry Johnnie," said Andrews, a note of urgency in his voice. "Time's more important than ever before." Johnnie was expert at his job now, and it was a matter of a minute or two before the wire was down and Johnnie was back in the cab. "Now, Mr. Knight, let's see what *The General* can do. Forget the speed limit and give her all she's got. If we don't set a new record for the Kingston-Adairsville run, we'll be in a worse mess at Adairsville than we were at Kingston. A southbound freight should be waiting on the siding to give the right of way to a southbound passenger train. We've got to get through Adairsville before that passenger train arrives. Make that fire roar, Mr. Wilson."

"We'll roll her as she's never been rolled before," said Knight with a huge grin. He and Brown had been itching to push *The General* to the limit, and it was only Andrews' insistence on maintaining Fuller's schedule that had kept *The General* at moderate speeds. Knight opened the throttle and pressed the sand lever. Wilson heaped wood on the fire. Black smoke and a shower of sparks belched from the stack. Steam hissed as the pistons revolved the huge driving wheels. Pulling a light load, *The General* gained speed rapidly. Ten, twenty, thirty, forty miles per hour. *The General* rocked from side to side like a rowboat in heavy surf, and careened dizzily around the sharp curves.

The men in the engine bounced off each other and off the walls of the cab. Johnnie wrapped himself around the braking wheel of the boxcar to keep himself from being pitched to the embankment. He shuddered to think of the men being tossed about in the boxcar. The tortuous Western and Atlantic road had never been built for such speed, and with the rails worn thin by heavy war traffic, it was a miracle that the locomotive held the track. But hold the track *The General* did.

After a run of a few miles, the whistle signaled a stop. Johnnie didn't know the reason for the stop, but he spun his wheel in obedience to the signal. Sparks flew from the track. "Up you go again, Johnnie," called Andrews. Johnnie climbed over the tender, grabbed his tools, jumped to the ground, and shinnied the pole. Men poured from the boxcar and split into two groups. One group worked feverishly at lifting a rail; the other rapidly loaded sleepers onto the last car. A sense of urgency animated their efforts. Time was far more important than when they had torn up the track between Big Shanty and Acworth. One end of rail broke loose. "Hurry, boys, bend that rail," urged Andrews. The men pushed, pried, lifted. The sound of heavy breathing, the shouts of encouragement, the urgent voice of Andrews, the thud of sleepers, the wrenching noise as bolts were drawn from the ties — all reached Johnnie's ears. Then, without the slightest warning, came the sound he dreaded most to hear — the sound of a train whistle, distant but unmistakable. And it came not from the direction of Adairsville, but from Kingston. It could mean only one thing. They were pursued!

8.
Pursued!

Johnnie screamed, "They're after us again, Mr. Andrews."

"What do you mean?" Andrews couldn't believe it.

"There's a train behind us. I heard the whistle."

"Are you sure the whistle came from the south?"

"Yes, sir."

Since Johnnie's first warning to Andrews, the rail lifters had suspended operations. Apparently no one but Johnnie had heard the ominous sound. "Back to your work, boys," said Andrews sharply. "We must snap that rail before the pursuing train spots us. Johnnie, keep your eyes and ears open."

There it was again; long, drawn out, shrill. Everyone heard it this time. No need to drive the men now — they realized only too well that the lifting of the rail was a life-and-death matter. In a few minutes at most, the Southern train would be upon them. Johnnie shaded his eyes. A cloud of black smoke rose above the trees in the distance.

"Smoke," he shouted. The rail lifters heaved and strained. Slowly the track rose; then with a dull twang, it snapped, tumbling the soldiers down the embankment into the ditch.

"All aboard! Hurry!" sang out Andrews. The rail lifters scrambled to their feet, picked up the rail, and hurried to the boxcar. The other men threw on a final load of sleepers. Andrews strode toward the cab. Johnnie slid down the pole and hurried forward. *The General* was already moving when he grabbed the handrail and swung on.

"Who do you suppose is after us?" asked Wilson.

"Probably one of those suspicious trainmen at Kingston," was Brown's opinion.

Knight disagreed. "No, it's that blasted Fuller."

"Fuller? How could he get to Kingston? Last we saw of him he was shaking a fist at us only a mile or two from Big Shanty."

"Must've kept running till he met up with the section gang. Put the handcar on the track and poled it as far as *The Yonah*, then rode *The Yonah* into Kingston. I knew we should've smashed that old tub."

"How'd he get past the break in the track?"

"Must have spotted it in time or hit it so slowly that the handcar wasn't damaged."

"How'd he get *The Yonah* through that snarl at Kingston?"

"Didn't try to. Just shifted to another train,

most likely the Rome local. It was heading in the right direction."

"Well, anyway, we've blocked him here."

"Mebbe. But that didn't stop him before, and it may not this time either."

Alf Wilson joined in. "What a mess! Two overdue trains on the track ahead and a pursuing train on the track behind. We're right between the devil and the deep."

"Don't lose heart, boys," cautioned Andrews. "The game's not up as long as the authorities ahead of us don't get the alarm. And we'll see that they don't. Keep a sharp lookout, Johnnie."

Johnnie's boxcar post didn't exactly have all the comforts of home. The rain had subsided to a drizzle again, but the black smoke pouring from the stack was alive with sparks which stung Johnnie's cheek and burned holes in his jacket. Actually, the rain was a blessing; otherwise Johnnie might have become a human torch. As Knight opened the throttle wider and wider, Johnnie's perch became increasingly precarious. Forced to shield his eyes and to brush the sparks from his clothing, he had only one hand with which to cling to the breaking wheel. As the car rocked violently from side to side and seemed occasionally to teeter dangerously on one rail, Johnnie had all he could do to keep from being catapulted through space. But he clung desperately to his post.

At the rate *The General* was careening down the track, it would not take long to reach Adairsville and the next crisis. A few miles farther on, Knight began to slow down. Scattered houses appeared along the track; then the depot came in sight, and finally the siding. The freight was waiting. "Freight's on the siding," called out Johnnie.

"Good," said Andrews.

As *The General* slowed to a halt beside the string of cars, Johnnie gazed admiringly at the powerful freight locomotive. It looked even newer and shinier than *The General*. The name "Texas" was lettered in gold on the boiler.

There was the usual barrage of questions about Fuller and his train, the usual Andrews reply about the powder train, the usual retort about Mitchel's seizure of the Memphis-Charleston road, and Andrews' counter about obeying orders. This time Andrews had a few questions of his own: he was concerned about the southbound passenger train, now a half-hour overdue. But neither the freight conductor nor the stationmaster had any information.

"I've waited here long enough," said the conductor. "I'm heading for Kingston." He was quite within his rights: the Western and Atlantic rules required him to wait only thirty minutes for a following train before pushing off to the next station. Andrews nodded his approval. Knight opened his mouth to protest, but Brown motioned him to silence. The conductor continued, "Of course, you'll wait here till the passenger arrives. Tell the conductor he can pass me at Kingston."

"I'm an hour late already," replied Andrews. "I must get this powder through. Suppose the Yanks attack Beauregard — he hasn't powder enough for a three-hour fight. I can't wait here."

"I guess you're right. But you'll have to run at reduced speed and send a flagman ahead on every curve. If you collide with the down passenger, you'll blow yourself to kingdom come."

Andrews nodded. Johnnie was amazed at the Southern railroad man's readiness to believe their story. As the stolen train traveled farther north and reports of Mitchel's advance became more and more authentic, the powder story became increasingly absurd. Yet Andrews' unfailing presence of mind and his air of authority lulled suspicion now as it had so often earlier in the day. The conductor signaled his engineer; the freight pulled onto the same track and headed south for Kingston. *The General* moved out of Adairsville in the opposite direction.

Knight was in one of his sputtering moods. "We should have kept that train here, Mr. Andrews. They'll see the broken rail and turn back to follow us. That will give the Confederates a pursuing engine this side of the torn-up track."

"It's a chance we'll have to take, Mr. Knight," replied Andrews. "If we meet the passenger train before we reach Calhoun and have to back to Adairsville, I don't want the track blocked here. There's not room for three trains. And if we are forced into a fight, the fewer the enemy at Adairsville the better. Also, don't forget that the freight may be derailed by the break in the track. That will eliminate the freight as a pursuer and tie up the track for some time."

"Let's hope it works out that way," said Knight good-naturedly.

Andrews looked at his watch. "It's ten-forty-five, boys. Let's see. Nine miles to Calhoun. Non-stop, Mr. Knight. I expect to be in Calhoun by ten-fifty-four."

Knight blanched. "Nine miles in nine minutes? That's impossible!" Brown and Wilson stared openmouthed at their leader.

"Why? Can't *The General* do it?"

"Sure *The General* can do it, *if* she stays on the track."

"Then keep her on the track."

"Yes, sir." Knight shook his head doubtfully.

"That flagman's sure gonna have a hard time running ahead of us on the curves," laughed Brown.

"Good job for you, Will," observed Alf.

"We may have to stop in a hurry," continued Andrews. "Be ready to shove her into reverse, Mr. Knight. Mr. Wilson, you operate the tender brakes. Mr. Brown, you better man the braking wheel on the second boxcar. That will give us an additional brake."

"If we meet that passenger between here and Calhoun, we'll have to set a world's record for braking or we'll all be sproutin' angels' wings," observed Knight wryly.

"More probably devils' tails," remarked Wilson. "Thieves don't go to heaven."

"Suppose we do meet the passenger train?" asked Knight.

"We try to persuade the conductor to back to Calhoun," replied Andrews.

"If he won't?"

"Then we try another method of persuasion." Andrews tapped his breast pocket.

Brown clambered over the tender and made his way past Johnnie and along the catwalk to the second car. "Hold on tight," cautioned Johnnie.

The General was rapidly gaining maximum speed. Wilson, dousing each stick of wood with oil, had a magnificent fire roaring. The heat from the firebox was almost unbearably intense. The men in the cab stripped off their jackets, but still perspiration poured down their faces. The cab rocked violently from side to side, and the Union soldiers were danced about like popcorn on a hot griddle.

Showers of sparks flew up as the huge drivers bit at the rails. Smoke and live embers poured from the stack — Johnnie was smoking like a chimney. He had never known such exhilaration. This race against time was really a contest between life and death. Although they had made every possible preparation for braking the stolen train, there was actually little chance of avoiding a collision if they met the down passenger between Adairsville and Calhoun. And collision could only result in certain death as well as the complete destruction of both trains. But with a pursuit organized in their rear, and the southbound freight heading for the broken rail between Adairsville and Kingston, they had no alternative to their breakneck speed. They simply had to reach Calhoun before the passenger train left. Fortunately, the Adairsville-Calhoun run was straight and level; if a mile a minute could be made without disaster anywhere on the Western and Atlantic, it could be made there.

Johnnie strained his eyes — alertness on his part might make the difference between disaster and success. At every curve the scream of the whistle rent the air. Andrews kept his eyes on his watch. "Doing fine, Mr. Knight. You are about to set a new record for the Adairsville-Calhoun run." Houses began to dot the countryside — they must be nearing Calhoun. Johnnie shaded his eyes. Yes, there was the depot and, bearing down upon them, a locomotive!

"Calhoun!" Johnnie yelled. "Locomotive heading toward us."

The whistle shrieked; Johnnie, Wilson, and Brown frantically set their brakes. The wheels locked; sparks flew from the track. Knight pushed the throttle to neutral and threw *The General* into reverse. The huge drivers rapidly decelerated and then began to revolve in the opposite direction, fighting against the forward motion of the engine. Brown raced back to apply the brakes on the last car. With all wheels locked or reversed, the stolen train slid screeching toward the passenger locomotive. Warned by the whistle and alarmed by the rapid approach of *The General*, the Confederate engineer had reversed his train and was now backing slowly toward the Calhoun station. Johnnie held his breath. Ahead he could see the siding and the switch tender standing by his switch. The stolen train slowed rapidly and the passenger gradually gained speed, but the gap between the two engines narrowed steadily until only twenty yards of track separated them. As the backing engine cleared the junction, the quick-thinking tender threw the switch. Still gaining on the other locomotive, *The General* lurched sharply to the left, then headed down the side track past the cars backing on the main line. The men in the cab tumbled in a heap; only a frantic grab at the braking wheel saved Johnnie from being pitched off the catwalk. When he recovered himself, *The General* had shuddered to a halt at the northern end of the siding. The passenger was standing motionless on the main track, its last car blocking the switch in front of *The General*. Andrews snapped his watch shut. "Seven and a half minutes, Mr. Knight. Nobody will beat that record for a long time to come."

The conductor of the passenger train strode toward *The General*. He was quivering with rage and fright. "Waddya tryin' to do? Kill us all?" he sputtered. "Don't you know the rules of the road? Speed limit eighteen miles per hour. My train has the right of way between here and Adairsville. Where was your flagman?" The conductor paused to catch his breath.

"My humblest apologies, sir," said Andrews. "I'm no more anxious to die than you are. But I'm running powder to General Beauregard and I'm behind schedule. Powder won't do Beauregard any good unless it gets to him in time."

"It won't do him any good if it never gets to him at all, either. You pull any more stunts like this and you'll never live to tell the tale. I ought to report you to the authorities."

Andrews was becoming a little exasperated. "I don't care what you do. Just clear the switch so I can move onto the main line."

The conductor was in no mood to cooperate. "Blamed if I will. Western and Atlantic's not safe any more with fools like you loose on the tracks. Fuller's probably heading this way with the mail.

I've just missed one collision and I'm not going to risk another."

"Fuller has orders to wait for you at Adairsville. You'll tie up the whole line if you wait here."

"I'd rather tie up the line than smash my train."

"You can stay here as long as you like as far as I'm concerned. Just move your train and clear the switch."

"I won't budge. I'm going to keep you here till Fuller comes. He'll know what to do with you." The conductor turned to go. Andrews blocked his way.

"See here, sir. I order you to move that train." With his left hand, Andrews whipped out the order from General Beauregard; his right hand rested on the butt of the pistol in his breast pocket. At the sight of Beauregard's signature, the conductor swallowed hard. Still sputtering, he turned and walked toward the head of his train.

Andrews mopped his brow. "Let's move on," he said anxiously. "We haven't cut wire since Kingston. Stop as soon as possible after we leave here, Mr. Brown." Brown was now at the throttle. The down passenger moved ahead, then stopped. As soon as the switch was set, Brown eased *The General* forward. "Johnnie," called Andrews, "tell the boys we lift a rail and load ties at the next stop. With the wires down and the track torn, we should have no further trouble. There are no more southbound trains to be passed. We'll have a clear track ahead and an obstructed track behind. The Confederates will have no way to block us from the north or follow us from the south. Then we start bridge burning. The Oostanaula Bridge is about five miles away." As the stolen train pulled onto the main line, Johnnie scampered back to relay Andrews' instructions. He noticed that the passenger train still had not left the station. His message delivered, Johnnie returned to his post.

About a mile from Calhoun, Brown halted *The General* near the end of a long curve. In an instant Johnnie was out of the cab and up the pole. Andrews, silk hat once more replaced by railroad cap, strode rapidly to the rear of the train. Men tumbled out of the boxcars and ran after Andrews. One group began loading the sleepers which would be used to kindle a fire in the Oostanaula Bridge. Another group gathered around Ross, who vigorously applied his crowbar to the rail joint. This rail resisted their efforts even more stubbornly than the first two. Slipping and sliding on the muddy ground, Ross pounded, pried, pushed, and lifted, but the rail refused to budge. Impatiently, Andrews wrested the bar from the Sergeant. He worked as if possessed by a demon. The track rose slightly. At the other end of the section, the soldiers clumsily and ineffectually attacked the track with a fence post. At Andrews' end, the track rose another inch or two. Andrews yielded the bar to

Ross. "Give it everything you have, Sergeant," he pleaded. "We've got to raise this rail." Ross lifted the bar shoulder high, then stood as if paralyzed. All along the track the Union soldiers froze. This time everyone heard it, loud, clear, and menacing — the whistle of a pursuing train!

9.
Pittenger Has a Plan

Ross let the crowbar fall dejectedly to his side. But Andrews recovered quickly. "Don't stop now, man! Fall to! Get that rail up!" Atop the pole, Johnnie looked south. Rising above the trees in the distance and pushing rapidly forward was a plume of black smoke. "Train smoke," called Johnnie. "Moving toward us fast."

Several men sprang to Ross's side, but under their utmost efforts the track still refused to bend or break or snap loose from the ties. "She won't give," grunted Ross.

"Raise her another inch or two. Bring that fence post here," ordered Andrews. Pittenger ran up. "Place it under the track. Maybe that will serve the purpose. All aboard!"

After inserting the fence post under the rail so as to raise it several inches above the level of the adjoining track, the men broke for the cars. Johnnie slid down the pole and ran to the cab. Brown opened the throttle; the drivers spun on the track and then caught hold; *The General* jerked forward. To the rear, the plume of smoke continued to advance above the trees lining the long bend in the track.

"Who's after us now?" asked Wilson.

"The passenger train. The conductor was suspicious enough," suggested Brown.

"Not him," remarked Knight. "He was too scared to move."

"*The Texas?*" Brown tried again.

"Sure," agreed Knight, "with Fuller at the throttle."

"Fuller! What would he be doing with *The Texas?* You've got Fuller on the brain," snorted Wilson.

"You mean Fuller's got us on the brain," retorted Knight. "He probably met *The Texas* at the broken track, backed it to Adairsville, dropped the boxcars there, and took after us with the locomotive and tender. That man's a bulldog."

Andrews broke in, "Any sign of the train, Johnnie?"

"No, sir." Johnnie had been watching the track carefully. The plume of smoke continued its rapid advance behind the trees. Any minute now the locomotive might burst into view. Yes, there it was, thundering around the bend. "Here they come," Johnnie sang out. "Locomotive and tender, tender first. Man sitting on the tender."

"Fuller," said Knight decisively.

"Keep us posted, Johnnie," ordered Andrews. As far as Johnnie could judge, the Confederates were only a few hundred yards from the partly lifted rail. Apparently they had not spotted the break, for the locomotive surged ahead with no reduction in speed. Johnnie held his breath. As if bent on self-destruction, the Southern train rushed madly onward. Suddenly the engine listed violently toward the outside of the curve, poised perilously on the portside wheels, then righted itself. The man on the tender shot into the air, landed sprawlingly athwart the roof of the cab, but managed miraculously to hang on.

"They made it," reported Johnnie.

"How did they do it?" asked Brown.

"Which rail did you lift, the inside or outside?" Knight turned to Andrews.

"Inside," answered Andrews.

"That explains it. Going around a curve, the weight is on the outside rail. If we'd lifted that rail, we'd have wrecked them sure."

"What do we do now?" asked Wilson.

No one had an answer. Andrews was absorbed in thought. Gloom hung heavy in the cab. Success in wrecking the Confederate train at this point would undoubtedly have blocked pursuit for good. In the past when they had torn up track, there had always been trains ahead of the break which could be mobilized for the chase. But now there were no trains ahead. If they could only have eliminated

110

this last engine, the success of their mission would have been assured.

Andrews broke the silence. "When we get to the top of the next grade, we'll uncouple the last car and back it toward their engine. If we can give it enough momentum, maybe it will accomplish what the lifted rail failed to do. Mr. Knight, you operate the brake on the second car and then uncouple. Johnnie, tell the boys to punch holes through to the last car and shift the sleepers into the second car."

Knight carefully made his way along the catwalk, as Johnny crawled back to deliver Andrews' message. Almost immediately the dull thud of the iron crowbar against the wooden wall of the boxcar revealed that Andrews' orders were being carried out. In a short time the Union soldiers had cut a hole into the second car large enough for them to crawl through. That done, they attacked the rear wall of the middle car.

Unfortunately for Andrews' plan to use a boxcar as a projectile, *The General* was running on a lengthy level stretch. But, not daring to wait longer and wishing to wreck or delay the pursuing train before they reached the Oostanaula Bridge, Andrews signaled a halt. Brown sounded the whistle and threw *The General* into reverse. Wilson set the tender brakes; Johnnie and Knight the boxcar brakes. The other men continued to pound their way to the last car. As *The General* screeched to a halt, Knight dropped to the ground and stepped between the last two cars. Sleepers were already being passed from the third to the second car. Knight straightened up from the coupling, waved to Andrews, and swung on. Men jumped from the last car and piled into the middle one, as the stolen train, rapidly gathering momentum, rushed toward the pursuing engine. Heedless of the impending danger, the Confederates drove forward at full speed. Then, as they sensed Andrews' maneuver, they attempted to avert disaster by stopping and reversing. Slowly the Confederate locomotive decelerated. Closing the gap as narrowly as he dared, Andrews lifted his hand. Brown pulled the whistle cord, released the reverse lever, and pushed the sand valve. The brakemen spun their wheels. As *The General* slowed, the boxcar hurtled toward the Southern train like a shot from a cannon. The pursuing engine screeched to a standstill, then began slowly to move in reverse. *The General*, drivers biting at the track, pulled gradually away. Swiftly the boxcar ate up the intervening distance. But as the Confederate locomotive gained momentum, the gap closed more slowly. With the issue still in doubt, the stolen train rushed around a curve. The boxcar and the pursuing train disappeared from view.

"Wonder if they'll back out of the way in time," said Brown.

"Probably," remarked Knight pessimistically.

"We'll soon see anyhow," observed Brown.

As *The General* rounded the curve, a long straight-away stretched before them. A mile ahead lay the Oostanaula Bridge, a covered wooden structure which they had counted on firing. "Light some sticks and branches, Mr. Wilson. Sing out, Johnnie, if you see our pursuers." Wilson opened the firebox and raked out a scoopful of glowing embers. Soon he had a set of torches ready to ignite the bridge. The rain had begun to fall heavily again, and it would take time to fire the rain-soaked timbers, more time than they would have if the Confederates had escaped the hurtling boxcar. Now the bridge was only a few hundred yards away. Anxiously Johnnie looked back at the long curve behind them. Suddenly the boxcar shot into view, propelled by the Confederate engine.

"There they are," shouted Johnnie. "They're pushing the boxcar."

"Blast them!" muttered Andrews. "Stop on the covered part of the bridge, Mr. Brown. Apply your brakes, Johnnie, and tell Mr. Knight to uncouple the rear car. Have the men move all the ties to the forward car. Throw those torches on the roof, Mr. Wilson."

Throttle in neutral and brakes set, *The General* thundered over the long trestle and came to rest in the middle of the covered bridge. The pursuing engine pressed ahead down the straightaway. Johnnie and Wilson raced back to throw the torches on the roof. Knight uncoupled the rear car, now empty of sleepers, and then ran forward. "If we derail this car, then the Johnny Rebs won't be able to add it to their train and push it along," he suggested.

"We haven't time for that," answered Andrews.

Ross walked up. "Let's stand and fight. We outnumber them. The covered bridge makes a perfect ambush."

Andrews shook his head. "We're too close to Resaca. The sound of gunfire will bring the whole town down on us." His shoulders sagged wearily. "All we can do is leave the car here and pray that in the darkness the enemy won't see it in time to prevent a collision. All aboard. Roll her, Mr. Brown."

As *The General* burst into the open again, Johnnie looked back and saw that the torches had not caught on. The thoroughly soaked timbers and the still falling rain had smothered the flames. Johnnie's heart sank. They were having an incredible streak of bad luck. Nothing they tried worked. Everything, even the weather, seemed against them. He had to admit that Knight and Ross were right — the day's delay had been fatal. On Friday they would have had dry weather and would have experienced no difficulty in burning the bridge. On Friday, the track would not have been clogged with southbound extras and they would not have suffered the catastrophic wait at Kingston that gave the Johnny Rebs time to organize a pursuit. On Friday, they mightn't have had Fuller to contend with. On Friday, Andrews' well-laid plans would have worked perfectly. But this was Saturday.

They rolled through Resaca without stopping. But as soon as the town was out of sight, Andrews ordered a halt, fearing that their pursuers, if they had passed through the bridge safely, might stop at Resaca to telegraph ahead. "Cut that wire, Johnnie," he commanded. "Load those ties," pointing to a pile of neatly stacked sleepers near the roadbed. "Ross, see what you can do with that bent rail we still have in the boxcar." The Union soldiers flew to obey Andrews' orders. Johnnie hoisted himself up the pole. George Wilson and Shadrack led a contingent to the pile of sleepers. Ross and Pittenger lugged the bent rail to the rear of the car. Placing one end underneath the track, they slanted the rail diagonally down the roadbed so that it thrust upward at a vicious angle toward any oncoming train.

Since leaving the Oostanaula, the train thieves had seen no sign of the pursuing engine and still did not know whether the boxcar had done its work on the bridge. But just as they had completed their assignments, the scream of a whistle smote their ears. Another scheme had failed. "Aboard," called Andrews, and once again the stolen train was under way.

Johnnie resumed his boxcar post and kept a sharp lookout to the rear. Soon the pursuing engine thundered around the bend and bore down on the bent rail. "Here they come again," Johnnie shouted. "Tender and locomotive alone."

"Must have sidetracked the boxcars at Resaca," observed Knight.

Once again the Confederates failed to see the obstacle on the track, but pushed their engine fearlessly at full speed. Johnnie breathed a silent prayer. This obstacle would have to work. Surely, all of their plans were not doomed to failure. Johnnie held his breath. The engine had reached the bent rail. His heart sank. With only a barely perceptible jolt, the engine passed over the obstruction and then rushed on unharmed.

"They made it again," he reported.

"Ross!" Andrews called out. Ross stuck his head through the jagged hole in the boxcar. "Have the men throw ties on the track. That will slow them up some. At least they won't dare to run full speed." Ross withdrew his head. Almost immediately ties began popping out through the hole in the rear of the boxcar. *The General* was now roaring down the track at forty miles per hour, and as the ties hit the roadbed they would leap about twenty feet into the air and shoot after the train, turning end over end like somersaulting gymnasts. Because of the speed of the train only a few remained on the track where they could cause trouble for the pursuing Confederates. But these few were enough to slow down the pursuit so that shortly the Southern train dropped from sight again.

"Wood's gettin' awful low, Mr. Andrews," reported Wilson.

Andrews nodded. "There's a wood station about five miles ahead. Push her, Mr. Brown. We need time to wood up."

Brown pulled back the throttle, and *The General* began another of its fearful races with time. Wilson opened the firebox and threw in the last armful of wood — the tender was empty of fuel. The fire now in the box would have to get *The General* to the wood station. The men in the cab were grim-faced. Andrews attempted to lighten the atmosphere. "Don't look so solemn, boys. We're not going to a funeral."

"Not unless it's ours," remarked Wilson dryly.

"Wood yard!" sang out Johnnie.

A minute or two later the entire band of raiders, except for Johnnie, who kept his post as lookout, converged on the woodpile. The need to conceal the size of the party was not so pressing as the need to load an adequate supply of fuel before their pursuers caught up with them again. The yard foreman looked suspiciously at the battered boxcar with both ends knocked out. "Fine-looking car, sir," remarked Andrews. "I'm running a special to General Beauregard. This is the best they could give me — rolling stock's scarce. Could you give us a hand? We're behind schedule."

"Glad to," assented the foreman. Johnnie gasped. How could he swallow such a story? Johnnie saw Andrews whisper a few words to Ross. Ross and two or three other men detached themselves from the loading detail and disappeared behind the boxcar. Johnnie peered anxiously down the track.

"Here they come," he called.

The tender was only half full. "Hurry, boys," urged Andrews. "We need more wood."

The Confederate train bore down upon them, whistle screaming intermittently. Trying to warn the foreman, thought Johnnie. The two trains were close enough now to raise the specter of a collision. The Confederate train slowed down — Johnnie could hear the brakes screech. "Aboard," commanded Andrews. The men broke for the train. All except Alf, who kept frantically heaping on more wood. *The General* inched forward.

"Come on, Alf," yelled Knight. Wilson threw on a final armful and leaped aboard. As the stolen train moved away from the wood station, a barricade emerged from the shadow of the boxcar. So that's what Ross was up to. The enemy would have to clear the track. That would give *The General* a chance to build up a lead. Johnnie saw that the pursuing tender was covered with gray-clad soldiers. As their train halted behind the barricade, they jumped to the ground, leveled their guns, and fired. But the distance was too great for accuracy — the bullets whizzed harmlessly past the fleeing *General.*

"We'll need some water soon," observed Knight, looking at the water gauge. "Boiler's getting mighty low."

"All right. We'll stop at the water tank on the other side of Tilton," answered Andrews.

The stolen train passed through Tilton without incident and stopped at the water tank outside the town limits. Once again the powder story was told and once again, to Johnnie's amazement, was swallowed whole. The foreman gladly swung the hose over to Johnnie, who inserted it into the tank. As the water rushed into the tender, the gauge in the cab rose steadily. "Quarter full. Half full," sang out Knight. "Three quarters — " The scream of a whistle drowned out his voice. The Confederate engine was upon them again.

"Do we have enough?" asked Andrews calmly.

"Plenty," replied Knight.

Andrews signaled the foreman. Johnnie removed the hose and replaced the manhole cover. Once again a barricade materialized as the stolen train moved away. Ross and his barricade raisers had been quietly and secretly at work while the foreman had been preoccupied with the hose.

Andrews looked at his watch and ran his finger down his timetable. "Eleven-thirty. We've nearly made up the hour we lost at Kingston. Dalton's eight miles from here. It's a rail junction like Kingston, and we may be held up there. We'd better have another try at rail lifting. The barricade back at the water station ought to give us time."

Around the first long curve, Andrews signaled a halt and then divided his men into four details. Johnnie went up the pole to cut wire. Brown and Knight carefully oiled and inspected the engine. George Wilson and the largest group attacked the rail, making certain this time to work on the outside of the curve. Ross and his barricaders ran back to erect an obstruction on the track beyond gunshot range of the rail lifters. If the pursuing train were halted this far away, the rail lifters might be given a few precious moments in which to complete their task. George Wilson and his men went at the rail with all their strength and cunning, but their clumsy tools made little headway. Observing this, Pittenger suddenly turned and walked toward Andrews.

"Mr. Andrews," he said, "I think I know how to capture the Southern train, if you're willing."

10.
The End of the Line

Andrews looked sharply at Pittenger. "What is your plan, Corporal?"

"Find a curve where there are plenty of bushes and trees along the roadbed. Build a barricade there and hide all of your men, except one engineer, in the underbrush. Have the engineer run *The General* ahead out of sight. When the Johnny Rebs stop to clear the track, we rush on them before they have time to get their muskets ready. After we have captured the locomotive, our second engineer sends it back down the track at full speed to clear the road of any other pursuing trains. Then our first engineer reverses *The General* to pick us up."

Andrews paused as if weighing the plan in his mind. "That might work, Corporal. It's worth a try. We'll chance it if the opportunity arises." The screech of a whistle interrupted any further discussion of Pittenger's plan. Ross and his party left the barricade and hurried back to get out of gun range. From the top of the pole, Johnnie saw the pursuing locomotive halt just short of the barricade. Men jumped to the ground and began working frantically to clear the track.

"Making any headway?" Andrews asked the rail lifters.

"No, sir, she won't budge," replied George Wilson wearily.

"Let's go then."

Back in the cab Andrews instructed Knight, who now had the throttle, to make all possible speed to Dalton. "It's the biggest city since Marietta, with a complicated series of switches as well as the junction of the East Tennessee and Georgia track from Knoxville. There are any number of ways we can be held up. We must get there well ahead of our pursuers. Sergeant Ross!" Ross stuck his head through the jagged hole in the boxcar. "Keep throwing ties on the track. Johnnie! Sing out at the first sign of Dalton."

Johnnie glanced hurriedly toward the rear of the train. No sign of the pursuing engine. Already the sleepers were popping from the boxcar, bouncing on the track, and leaping high into the air. A few stayed on the roadbed; enough, he hoped, to enable *The General* to outdistance the Confederate train. Knight had the throttle wide open. Without the steadying weight of the second and third cars, the stolen train rocked and reeled more terrifyingly than on the mad dash from Adairsville to Calhoun. The men in the cab clung to the stanchions. Johnnie wrapped himself round the brake rod. He could hear the soldiers in the boxcar slamming against the wooden walls.

At this fearful speed, it was only a matter of minutes before the outskirts of Dalton came into view. "Dalton!" Johnnie shouted above the clatter of the train. Knight threw the throttle into neutral and pushed the reverse lever. Johnnie and Brown spun the braking wheels. Sparks flying from the rails, *The General* skidded to a screeching halt. The train still in motion, Andrews dropped off and ran ahead a hundred yards or so to where the East Tennessee and Georgia joined the Western and Atlantic. Another hundred yards ahead was the depot, a large tunnellike structure which extended clear over the track. As Andrews reached the junction, the dreaded whistle sounded from the south. Andrews inspected the switch, signaled to Knight, then dashed back toward *The General*, brushing off one or two railroad men who hurled questions at him. As *The General* moved forward, Andrews swung breathlessly aboard.

"Full speed ahead," he panted. "Main switch is set for us. No time to check the other switches!"

The General rushed at the depot and roared into the darkness under the roof. A wave of black smoke engulfed the cab. Cinders and hot embers stung Johnnie's cheek. Suddenly the train veered sharply to the left. Nearly pitched from his post,

Johnnie had an awful moment of panic — he was sure that *The General* had crossed over a closed switch and was headed for certain destruction. But the train righted itself and burst into daylight. They were careening down the main line!

A moment or two later the braking whistle sounded. Johnnie set his brakes. He heard Andrews explaining to Knight that the first of the Chickamauga bridges was just ahead. He wanted the track obstructed and a rail lifted so as to allow time to kindle the bridge. Also the wire must be cut, since the people at Dalton, their suspicions aroused by the mad flight of *The General,* would certainly telegraph ahead.

Ross and his barricaders went to work. George Wilson and his party attacked the rail. Johnnie was up the pole in a flash. It was not until he reached the top that he saw something that nearly sent him plunging to the ground. Only a few hundred yards away encamped in a field was a Confederate regiment. In the excitement of the moment, Andrews had completely failed to notice the camp. Johnnie screamed and pointed. Andrews shrugged his shoulders. Too late to do anything about it now! Johnnie cut the wire and dropped to the embankment. Ross worked steadily at the barricade, Wilson at the outside rail. To Johnnie's amazement, the soldiers in the camp paid no attention to them. Then the dreadful whistle sounded again. Thwarted once more. "All aboard," yelled

Andrews. The soldiers scrambled into the boxcar. Johnnie resumed his post. *The General* shot forward.

Fields and houses rushed by. The wires rose and fell, rose and fell, with rapid monotony. Johnnie peered ahead. Before him rose a high mountain. The track disappeared into a tunnel, which Johnnie could see as a round black hole in the side of the hill. Judged by the height of the mountain, the tunnel must be a long one. The ideal place for an ambush! A glorious chance to try Pittenger's plan!

"Tunnel ahead," Johnnie called out.

Pittenger and Ross peered over the tender. "How about my scheme, Mr. Andrews?" asked Pittenger.

Andrews hesitated.

"Couldn't ask for a better spot for an ambush," Pittenger continued.

"Or for a train wreck," added Ross.

"Or both," said Pittenger. "If we build a barricade, they may not see it in the dark until it's too late to stop. If they slow down, or stop, or are wrecked, we can fall upon them before they can get organized. At close quarters our pistols will be handier than their rifles."

"And our eyes will be used to the dark," stuck in Ross. "Theirs won't be. We can pick them off before they even see us."

"Sounds good to me," said Knight.

"I'm for it," agreed Brown.

125

"Looks like our last chance," observed Wilson.

Andrews was tempted. But finally he shook his head. "No, boys. Our mission is to wreck the Western and Atlantic. That means bridge burning. Our immediate objective is the first Chickamauga Bridge."

"But," protested Pittenger, "we'll never burn a single bridge until we eliminate that engine."

Andrews shook his head again. "I can't stake everything on an ambush. If the ambush fails, then our mission fails. The way things are now, we still have a chance with the next bridge. Sergeant" — Andrews' voice had the old ring of authority — "kindle a fire in the boxcar. We'll drop the car in the middle of the bridge and use it as a torch."

"Yes, sir." Ross gathered an armful of wood and disappeared into the boxcar. The sound of an ax told Johnnie that Andrews' orders were being carried out. In a moment, Ross's head reappeared. "We need some live coals and some burning twigs." Wilson opened the firebox, scraped out a scoopful of coals and a few blazing sticks, and passed them to Johnnie. Johnnie handed the scoop to Ross. Wilson picked up the oilcan.

"Give this to Ross, but tell him to take it easy. It's all we have." Johnnie passed the can into the boxcar.

Suddenly darkness descended on the cab — *The*

General had entered the tunnel. A feeble flicker in the boxcar showed that Ross had a fire started, although a small one. Like everything else on this miserable day, the boxcar was thoroughly soaked and its soggy timbers caught fire with agonizing slowness. Johnnie could hear the soldiers blowing on the fire and fanning the embers with their coats. Gradually the flames rose and when the stolen train burst into daylight, Ross had a lusty blaze going. As *The General* rumbled through the village of Tunnel Hill at slightly reduced speed, smoke and steam were beginning to rise from the boxcar. Platform passengers stared bewilderedly at the smoking, hissing car with the jagged holes in each end. This time there was no wire-cutting stop — Andrews was saving every precious second for the firing of the bridge. The rain fell relentlessly, but the flames gained ground. One by one, forced out by the heat of the fire, Ross's men emerged from the boxcar and crowded onto the tender. Soon the tender was a mass of men, with only Ross remaining behind to encourage the flames.

Rain beating in his face, Johnnie peered ahead, eyes alert for the bridge. Just as Ross joined his comrades on the tender, the covered wooden structure came in sight. "Bridge ahead," called out Johnnie.

"Brakes!" shouted Andrews.

The General clattered over the long, high trestle and stopped in the center of the bridge.

"Uncouple, Mr. Brown. Throw all the wood on the boxcar fire, boys. Any oil left, Mr. Wilson?" Wilson nodded. "Pour it on."

Ross was examining the roof of the bridge. "Dry enough on the inside. She'll burn if given time."

Time! Time had been the vital factor all day. But at no point in the raid had it been so vital as now. Andrews had staked his all on one last desperate gamble. The tender had been emptied of wood to feed the flames in the boxcar; the locomotive would have to make the next wood yard on the steam now in the boiler. If the bridge ignited quickly and thus blocked pursuit, *The General* could limp to the wood yard. But if not, then the pursuing engine would pass safely through and rapidly overhaul the stolen train. Johnnie knew this, and he could see in the tense, strained faces of his comrades that they knew it, too. Each man kept one eye on the flaming boxcar, the other on the track to the south. Shielded from the downpour, the car was now blazing briskly. The flames licked at the roof greedily, but the rain-drenched eaves yielded reluctantly. Here and there the timbers caught fire. Ross was right — given time. . . .

But time was not given. In the distance, Johnnie's keen young eyes saw the dreaded plume of smoke rise above the trees. "Train smoke to the south," he warned.

"That does it," said Wilson in a disconsolate whisper.

The raiders looked despairingly at the steaming eaves. Just a little more time!

"All aboard, boys," commanded Andrews tonelessly. The soldiers clambered dispiritedly onto the tender. *The General* puffed wearily out of the bridge and into the driving rain. Brown looked back at the smoldering bridge.

"They'll push the boxcar ahead and drop it at the next siding," he remarked dejectedly. "The bridge won't burn without the car as kindling."

A mile or two beyond the bridge, the stolen train chugged through Ringgold. The men on the tender crouched down as best they could so as not to attract too much attention.

"Where's the next wood yard?" asked Knight.

"One mile this side of Graysville. Four miles from here," answered Andrews.

"We'll never make it," said Knight.

"We'll try," said Andrews. "We'll throw in everything we have." Suiting his action to his words, he stripped off his coat and handed it to the fireman. Other members of the party did likewise. Soon Wilson was stuffing his firebox with an odd assortment of clothing. Given this new lease on life, *The General* picked up speed. But the spurt was short lived, and the worn-out locomotive sputtered, coughed, and wheezed.

"It's no go," said Knight. "We need wood."

"Water and oil, too," remarked Brown. "The brass on the journals is beginning to melt."

Andrews said nothing. Silently he handed a sheaf of papers to Wilson. The order from General Beauregard followed, then the Western and Atlantic timetable, finally the railroad cap. Andrews was destroying all incriminating evidence. Wilson opened the firebox and threw in the cap and the papers.

"Well, boys," said Andrews, "this is the end of the line. You've been all that a leader could ask. You have followed me loyally, courageously, resourcefully. We have occasionally disagreed on strategy, but you have spoken up like brave men and then carried out my orders to the best of your ability. We have failed through no fault of yours. The day's delay ruined our plans. Yesterday we would have succeeded."

Andrews pulled out his watch. "It's two o'clock, boys. We're about a mile from Graysville and nineteen from Chattanooga. The best plan is for us to scatter into small groups and make our way separately toward the Union lines."

"Mr. Andrews," interrupted Ross, "wouldn't it be better for us to stick together? We make a strong armed party. If we keep to the woods and the mountains, they'll have difficulty organizing quickly a posse large enough to take us." Here again was the conflict between the soldier accustomed to direct action and to working with a body of disciplined men and the secret agent accustomed to subtle stratagem and to working alone.

"I think not, Sergeant," resumed Andrews. "It's very likely that the size of our party is not yet generally known. Except for the water tender at Tilton, the enemy have seen only the men in the cab. Undoubtedly not all of us will make the Union lines. But after a few are captured, the search may be given up. The rest of us may then slip through. A large group is bound to excite suspicion. Singly or in small groups you may get by."

Andrews paused. "One last word of caution, boys. Conceal your identities as long as you can. But if you are recognized, give your name and unit. Be sure to state that you were compelled to take part in a military raid, but that you were under sealed orders and that you have taken no lives. I guess that's all, boys. I thank you again for your courage and your loyalty."

Ross jumped into the cab from the tender. "Mr. Andrews, you mentioned our little squabbles. I guess no one argued more than I did. But I want you to know, and I'm sure I speak for all of the men, that it's been an honor to serve with you."

Andrews took Ross's extended hand. There were tears in his eyes. "Thank you, Sergeant."

The scream of a whistle rent the air. "I'll lead the way," said Ross. He saluted and jumped to the ground. Over and over, he rolled down the embankment. Gaining his feet, he waved at the slowly moving *General*, turned, and ran across the field to the woods. One by one the other raiders followed Ross's example, each pausing to shake hands with Andrews before he leaped.

Johnnie looked back. The Southern engine was bearing down upon them. *The General* was rapidly losing speed, as the steam pressure dropped toward the zero mark. In the sky, the sun had suddenly broken through the clouds. Fine time, thought Johnnie. Well, anyway, the woods may dry up a bit.

Andrews was talking to Knight. "As soon as they've all jumped, shove *The General* into reverse and back her toward the Southerners. That will give us a little extra time."

"Yes, sir," said Knight.

Now it was Johnnie's turn. Andrews put his arm around Johnnie's shoulders. "Good-bye, Johnnie. You're a brave lad. Keep your chin up and your wits about you. You've the best chance of any of us. You don't look like a desperate character." Andrews smiled. "Good luck, Johnnie."

Johnnie choked up. He hated to leave Andrews, and he hated to leave the sturdy old *General*. "Good-bye, Mr. Andrews," he said and leaped from the cab.

11.
Down the Tennessee River

As Johnnie shot through the air, he began moving his legs like pistons so that when he hit the ground he was able to maintain his forward motion without losing his balance. In a split second he was over the fence and running full speed across the field. Reaching the woods, he looked over his shoulder. The backing *General* wheezed down the track. The Confederates had reversed their engine — Johnnie wondered if it were *The Texas* — and were having no trouble keeping a safe distance. Then, with a sigh and a shudder, *The General* stopped dead. Poor old engine, thought Johnnie. Civilians and gray-clad soldiers poured from the Confederate train, fanned out, and made for the woods. In the field below, Johnnie could see Knight and Andrews running through the tall grass. They must have been the last to jump. There was no sign of the rest of the party. One or two Confederate soldiers knelt and fired. Johnnie heard the whine of bullets, but Knight and Andrews kept on. They weren't hit.

Johnnie plunged into the woods. For what seemed like an eternity he worked his way through the underbrush, tripping on roots, clawing branches and vines from his face. The rain-drenched foliage soaked his clothing from head to foot. His knees grew weak, his breath came in gasps, his heart pounded against his ribs, but still he kept on. Suddenly his foot caught on a root; he pitched headlong into a thicket and fell facedown on a smooth, level surface. He raised his head. He seemed to be in a cave whose entrance was screened by the underbrush through which he had tumbled. What luck, he thought; I can rest here without fear of discovery. He tried to rise, but collapsed weakly on his face. He suddenly realized he was faint from lack of food — he hadn't eaten since early that morning — as well as exhausted by his breathless dash through the forest. As he lay on the floor of the cave gasping for breath, exhaustion and faintness gradually overpowered him and he lost consciousness.

Several hours later Johnnie awoke with a start. He sat up. There was movement outside his cave. "Seen any of them?" Johnnie heard someone say.

"Nope, not a sign."

Johnnie was shivering from head to foot; his teeth clattered like castanets. Not so much from fear as from cold. He had sacrificed his coat to the firebox in the last futile attempt to keep *The General* rolling. The dampness of the cave and of Johnnie's clothes and the cool evening air chilled him to the bone. He bit his sleeve to stop the chattering of his teeth.

"What was that?" asked the first voice. Johnnie's heart sank — it seemed to him that his chattering teeth could be heard all over the state of Georgia.

"I didn't hear a sound. You're imagining things."

"What do we do now?"

"I don't know what you're going to do, but I'm through for the night. I don't go for moonlight manhunts in rain-drenched woods. I'm heading back to Graysville."

Johnnie breathed easier. The sound of voices died away; Johnnie could hear the two men threshing through the underbrush. He peered cautiously through the thicket, then stepped out and began hopping up and down and rubbing his arms to get a little warmth into his veins.

"I've got to get something to eat," he said half aloud, striking out vigorously in the opposite direction from that taken by the two Southerners. Three hours later, about eight o'clock Johnnie estimated, he came to a narrow, dusty road winding tortuously northward. He had had enough of tramping through the wet woods, so he decided to follow the road. A little farther on he saw a small cabin set back a hundred yards or so from the road. Without something to eat he felt he could go no farther. Even at the risk of recognition and capture he would have to ask for food. He went up the path and knocked. The door opened an inch; an old black man peered cautiously through the slit.

"I've lost my way. I haven't eaten since morning. Could you give me something? I can pay for it."

At the mention of money, the old man opened the door and Johnnie stepped into the poorly furnished one-room cabin. The man bustled about, took down some corn bread from a shelf on the wall, then opened a trapdoor in the floor and pulled up a pitcher of buttermilk. Johnnie ate ravenously — nothing had ever tasted so good. When he had finished, he placed one of his Confederate bills on the table. "That was mighty tasty. If you have anything else, I'd like to buy it and take it with me." The black man silently produced a platter of oatmeal cakes. Johnnie stuffed them into his pocket and handed the old man another bill. "I'm much obliged," said Johnnie, rising to go.

Out on the road again, Johnnie strode ahead with renewed energy. He thought it best to take advantage of the darkness to get as far as he could from the Western and Atlantic track while his strength held out. For several hours he walked on into the night. The chill evening breeze blew through his damp clothing until he was blue with cold. Feeling he could not stand the cold much longer, he began to look for shelter. Just as he was about to give up and collapse by the roadside, he spied a barn. The hayloft was full of warm, sweet hay. Johnnie quickly fashioned a bed, and covering himself with straw and an old burlap bag, he was asleep almost before he closed his eyes.

When Johnnie woke up, the sun was high in the sky. Must be ten o'clock, he guessed. Lucky no one found me. Better get out of here quick. He made his way cautiously to the road. Suddenly he remembered it was Sunday. That was why no one was around — everybody was probably at church. He nibbled an oatmeal cake as he walked along. He was careful not to eat too much; no telling how long he'd have to make the oatcakes last.

The morning passed without incident. But in mid-afternoon Johnnie heard a sound that struck terror to his heart — the baying of hounds. He looked back. On the road behind, a pair of men with a brace of hounds on leash were advancing rapidly. Panic seized him. He left the road, hurdled a fence, dashed across a meadow, and plunged into the forest. Then suddenly his self-possession returned. "You fool, Johnnie," he said aloud. "You shouldn't have done that. Gave yourself away. You should have stayed on the road. Remember what Andrews said — you look too young for a Yankee spy. Too late now." Johnnie hurled himself through the underbrush. "They must have seen me. I'll simply have to outdistance them."

But that was easier said than done. No matter

how hard he ran, Johnnie could not shake his pursuers. The baying of the hounds sometimes receded, sometimes grew louder, but never died away completely. This went on for over an hour. Johnnie felt himself grow weaker. How long could he hold out? The Southerners now seemed to be gaining steadily. Johnnie burst into a small clearing. At the far end was a brook. About twenty yards from the bank was a squat, leafy tree. A plan suddenly occurred to Johnnie. He raced for the tree and then for the brook. When he reached the bank, he turned round and raced back toward the tree, being careful to retrace his steps. Nearing the tree, he leaped into the air, grabbed the lowest branch, swung himself up, and in a trice was hidden in the leafy branches. All he could do now was stay still, wait, and pray that his plan would work. He hoped he wouldn't have to sneeze. In a moment or two the men and the dogs appeared at the edge of the clearing. The dogs, straining at the leash, tugged the two men past the tree to the brook. So far so good, thought Johnnie. At the bank, the dogs paused, looked at their masters, and wagged their tails. One of the men led his dog to the opposite bank.

"Didn't cross here," he said.

"Must have taken to the water," remarked the other man.

"Which way?"

The second man paused. "Let's try downstream."

Giving the two men time to get out of earshot, Johnnie swung down, retraced his steps to the bank, and set off upstream in the middle of the brook. An hour later, having heard no sounds of pursuit, Johnnie sat down on a huge, flat rock and ate the rest of his oatmeal cakes. The sun was sinking in the west, a high wind was rising, and the rain was beginning to fall. His cakes finished, Johnnie splashed his way upstream again. The river bed became steeper and rockier, but Johnnie did not yet dare to risk a journey on land. He kept on doggedly, but his strength was ebbing fast. The cool of the evening, the high wind, the sheets of rain congealed the blood in his veins. I can't go on much more like this, he thought. So, when the brook ran under a narrow plank bridge, Johnnie decided to follow the road. He had to get food and find shelter from the cold and rain. A light shone ahead. Then a small frame house came in sight. He'd have to take the chance. In answer to his knock, the door opened to reveal a tall, dignified woman of middle age.

"Excuse me, ma'm. I've lost my way. I'm cold and hungry. Can you help me? I have some money."

The woman opened the door wider. Johnnie fell across the threshold. A strong hand guided him to a chair. Across the table stood a well-dressed man; a gun in his hand pointed at Johnnie's head.

"It's only a lad, Jim," the woman said. "He's wet to the bone. Put down your gun."

The man lowered his gun. "Heat him some broth, Mother." The woman hung an iron kettle over the fire. The man opened a door at the far end of the room. "Come in here, son," he said. "Take off your wet clothes. Put these on. They belong to our son. He's off at the war." He handed a change of clothes to Johnnie. Johnnie wondered which army their son was in, the blue or the gray. When he returned to the main room, the woman had a steaming bowl of broth ready for him. He ate greedily. They asked no questions, and he was too hungry and tired to talk. After he had finished his bowl, he was overcome by sudden drowsiness.

"You're tired, lad," said the man. "You can have our son's bed." This would be Johnnie's first sound sleep since leaving Shelbyville.

When Johnnie awoke the next morning, his host was standing by the bed. Over his arm were Johnnie's clothes. He looked steadily at Johnnie. "You're a Yankee, aren't you, son?"

Johnnie began a denial. "Don't deny it, lad. We won't turn you in. We're Union people. Our son's with Grant. You're one of the train thieves, aren't you?"

Johnnie nodded. Perhaps he shouldn't have, but he trusted the people who had sheltered him. "How did I give myself away?"

"You didn't, son. But we can spot a Yankee. And you fit the description of the boy who was seen on the stolen locomotive." Johnnie shuddered. "My name is Parsons."

During breakfast, Johnnie learned that he had made his way across the Georgia-Tennessee border west of Chattanooga and south of the Tennessee River. The whole countryside was up in arms and in search of the raiders. A few had been captured, but most were still at large. Johnnie gave an account of the raid and of his flight through the woods. At the end of breakfast Mr. Parsons said, "We have a place to hide you till dark. It isn't safe for you to travel during the daylight. We'll think of a way to get you back to Mitchel's army tonight."

It was barely daylight when Mr. Parsons led Johnnie out the rear of the house to an old abandoned barn set back from the road in a secluded spot. In the center of the floor was a trapdoor opening into a cellar hole about four feet square. "Here's where you spend the day, Johnnie. It's not very big, but it's dry and warm and safe. We'll bring you some lunch. By nightfall we'll have figured out a plan."

Johnnie could not stretch out full length, but by bunching some quilts he found, he made himself quite comfortable in a half-reclining posture. Waking, sleeping, dozing, wondering about the fate of his comrades, he made the time pass quickly enough. At sunset he was conducted back to the house. Around the supper table, Mr. Parsons outlined his scheme to get Johnnie back to the Federal Army. "I figure your best bet is to go by water. The Tennessee River is only a few miles from here, and I have a boat you can use. The current will float you toward the Union lines. You'll have to be on the watch for Southern units, and you may meet an enemy gunboat or two. But it promises to be a dark night, and I think your chances are better than on land. At least, you'll move faster and you can't get lost. Somewhere along the river you ought to spot a Union scouting party or cavalry patrol."

"Where's General Mitchel now?" Johnnie asked.

"Below Stevenson holding the Memphis-Charleston tracks. That's why you're bound to meet one of his units if you can get past the gunboats. Time to go, Johnnie."

Mrs. Parsons handed him a jacket. "You'll need this, Johnnie. It will be cold on the river."

Half an hour later Johnnie and his friend had reached the south bank of the Tennessee. From a thicket, Mr. Parsons drew a light, flat-bottomed skiff. Johnnie drew out the remainder of his Confederate money. "I'd like to pay you for the boat, the jacket, and the food." Mr. Parsons declined. "But it will soon be of no use to me," Johnnie insisted.

"All right. But you keep half. You may need it. You're not in Union territory yet. With luck you may be soon. Let's hope so. Watch out for the rapids."

Johnnie shook hands and pushed his boat from the bank. The current took hold and moved Johnnie slowly downstream. Soon Mr. Parsons was swallowed up by the darkness. For some time Johnnie rowed on in the stillness of the night. Then the throb of an engine warned him of an approaching vessel. Probably one of the Confederate gunboats, he thought, making rapidly for the shore. Pulling his skiff up on the bank, he watched the shadowy outline of a boat glide by. "Lucky I heard it. I'd never have seen it in time on a night like this," he muttered.

Johnnie's most anxious moments came when the river suddenly narrowed and rushed with frightening speed between two mountainous bluffs. It required all his agility and strength to keep the boat from capsizing or being dashed to pieces against the rocky cliffs. At times the skiff whirled around in dizzying circles; at others it shot like an arrow straight for one of the sheer granite walls rising from the river. But by standing in the bow and using one of his oars as a boat hook, Johnnie managed to ward off destruction. Then as suddenly as it had narrowed, the Tennessee broadened and the skiff burst from the maelstrom into peaceful lagoonlike water. Exhausted, Johnnie collapsed to the floor boards, letting the boat drift with the current.

Sometime later, Johnnie floated past what he guessed to be Bridgeport, the Alabama city where three days ago the Andrews raiders had expected to meet General Mitchel. The railroad bridge was a twisted mass of wreckage spiraling into the river. "Lucky for me," said Johnnie to himself. "The bridge might have been heavily guarded and difficult to get by."

Several hours passed without incident. Johnnie was beginning to get worried. He was tired, his hands were badly blistered, the sky was beginning to lighten, and still he had seen no sign of Union troops. Soon he would have to land and hide in the underbrush until the covering darkness of the following evening would make it safe for him to proceed. "I'll go on a little farther," he said half aloud. With the vigor of desperation, he plied his oars. His arms were heavy as lead and his hands were raw and bleeding, but still he rowed on and on. Suddenly he heard something. Was it the sound of horses' hoofs and the clatter of sabers? He looked ahead over his shoulder. Dimly he could see the outline of a bridge looming over the river, and on the northern shore the shadowy forms of men and horses. A cavalry unit! But were they wearing blue or gray? With his last reserve of strength he bent his back over the oars. The cavalry troop began filing over the bridge. Then for the first time since he had left Mr. Parsons, the moonlight broke through the clouds. Johnnie glanced over his shoulder again. The horsemen were clad in blue! Johnnie's scream pierced the still night air. "Wait a minute!" he yelled, heading his boat frantically for the south bank. A young lieutenant held up his hand. The troop halted. Johnnie's skiff hit the shore with a crunch and a jolt that pitched Johnnie over the bow and onto the muddy bank. He picked himself up, stumbled toward the cavalrymen, halted before the young lieutenant, came to attention, and saluted. "Private Johnnie Adams, Company C, Second Ohio," he said and fell in a heap at the lieutenant's feet.

Epilogue

Nearly a year later, on March 25, 1863, Johnnie Adams stood in the anteroom to President Lincoln's office in the White House. In the room with him were the surviving members of the Andrews raid, fifteen in number. As Johnnie looked about him, he saw the familiar faces — Brown, Knight, Pittenger, Alf Wilson, and others. But Andrews was not there; nor were Ross, Shadrack, and George Wilson. As he thought of the tragic death of these brave men, a lump rose in Johnnie's throat.

Of the entire band only Johnnie had succeeded in reaching the Union lines after the abandonment of *The General* near Graysville. The rest had been captured, chained, and thrown into Confederate prisons in Atlanta and Chattanooga. In June, Andrews and seven of his party had been hanged as spies. The following March, Brown, Knight, Alf Wilson, and four others had escaped and made their way to Federal-held territory. Pittenger and the five remaining raiders had been exchanged just six days before their reunion at the White House. They had all been summoned to Washington to meet the President and to receive Medals of Honor awarded by Congress to the survivors and to the families of those who had given their lives.

The raiders had many tales to swap. Johnnie told his admiring elders how he had used the Tennessee to reach the Union lines. Alf Wilson narrated his miraculous trip down the Chattahoochee River to Key West, where he had been rescued by the Federal fleet. Others had equally marvelous escape stories to tell. Pittenger described the horrors of the Confederate prisons in Richmond.

A door opened and in walked an efficient-looking young man — Johnnie guessed it was the President's secretary, John Hay. "The President will see you now." The Andrews raiders followed the secretary into the President's office. Mr. Lincoln rose to greet them.

"Good afternoon, gentlemen," he said. Johnnie gazed in awe at the tall, gaunt figure with the sad but kindly eyes. The President continued. "Congress has voted Medals of Honor to all participants in the Andrews raid. It is a great honor for me to present them to you personally. I deeply regret that the entire party has not survived to receive this expression of the country's gratitude. Congress has also authorized me to offer you commissions in the regular army. Should you wish to accept, Mr. Hay will take you to Mr. Stanton at the War Department.

"I have read of your raid with keen interest. Unquestionably one of the great exploits of this tragic war. What a pity General Mitchel didn't allow you boys another day to reach Marietta. Had he done so, I have no doubt you would have succeeded. But it was a brave attempt, and I am delighted that so many of you are here today."

Mr. Lincoln moved easily from man to man, shaking hands with each one and handing him the medal inscribed with the recipient's name. When he came to Johnnie, he said, "You must be Private Adams. So you're the lad who gave his elders a lesson in the technique of escape." The President smiled. Johnnie blushed. His comrades laughed.

Having spoken to each raider individually, Mr. Lincoln returned to his desk at the rear of the room. "I should like to talk further with you gentlemen, but I have many pressing matters to attend to, such as finding a leader who can beat General Lee. Possibly you gentlemen can suggest someone."

"There's General Grant," said Pittenger.

"Yes, but I need him in the West. Perhaps General Mitchel could have helped me if he had lived. I have many brave soldiers like yourselves, but no one to lead them properly." The sadness in the President's eyes deepened.

"Well, no need to burden you boys with my troubles. You have been granted sixty days leave. I hope you find your families well when you reach home. It has been a pleasure to meet you. Good day, gentlemen."

The interview was over. Mr. Hay opened the door. The Andrews raiders filed out.